Chapters

1 Destination London

2 Accommodation

3 Squatters

4 Crystal Palace

5 Feral

6 Sunny

7 Coming of Age

8 Coal-hole

9 Whirlwind

10 Twenty

11 Yogi

12 East end

13 Breakdown

14 Family

15 Manor Park Mark

16 Happy Birthday

17 Bed and Breakfast

18 New Life

19 Infidelity

20 Christmas

21 Scrubs

22 Breakup

23 Employment

24 Emptiness

Living On Empty

Following on from first book - **Slipping Through the Net**.

Foreword

Someone once said, 'When a man is tired of London, he's tired of life; for there is in London all that life can afford.' But that man didn't find himself living in London as the underclass do. Living in poverty, one cannot sample the variety of nightlife, restaurants and theatres which prevent a person being tired of London. Although one can always walk around and look at the river and the architecture as that's for free. But it's difficult to appreciate it all when you have nowhere appropriate to sleep at night or you feel the constant threat of homelessness.

Before we can appreciate, thrive and achieve in this world, our basic needs have to be met. For those who've never experienced the feeling of a lack of basics, this may be difficult to comprehend. We humans need a home or at the very least, a roof over our heads. In some cases, managing to get a permanent place to live becomes a huge achievement in itself. Even, the greatest achievement of a lifetime.

Assuming our basic needs are met, the question then is, should we be in pursuit of happiness in this life? Rather than the pursuit of happiness, I would suggest that it would be prudent to search for meaning in our short lives. The sensible prioritise purpose over the pursuit of happiness. I suppose searching for happiness is just too abstract.

The easiest walk is along the foot of the hills. But life is an uphill climb, so find a range of hills and aim to climb to the highest peak. Literally or metaphorically. There, you'll discover something better than happiness. And if moments of happiness come to you during your uphill climb or when you reach the peak, you should fall on your knees in gratitude.

Prologue

London is no place for vulnerable, unprotected girls. It's different for those who go there for collage or university. A plan is set in place with accommodation and a reason for being there. A backup of parents - a safety net.

I was seventeen, my parents had already set me up with my accommodation in London. A small bedsit, not far from the ballet school. Just a few stops on the underground train or tube as it was known. My brand new, pink leather cases were packed with my leotards, tights and several pairs of soft shoes and point shoes. All of my usual day-to-day stuff was in there too. Plus, trinkets and good-luck gifts from my relatives, friends and old Hollymount neighbours. My parents and sister were going to drop me off and of course Mum would make sure my new place was suitably clean and tidy. Then dad would take me food shopping and fill my tiny fridge. Then he'd insist I take some money from him, in case I needed it, £20! We'd be going for lunch, of course, my choice of restaurant, my sister knew I'd choose pizza! And I did and we all laughed. I didn't feel nervous or scared about my new life in the Big city. I was just full of excitement for going off to ballet school. I'd be seeing Mum, Dad and Carol, soon enough, back in Worcester in the summer holidays.

None of that was true. It was just a fantasy which I had as the cold wind brushed passed me. I was standing all alone on the train platform. Destination nowhere.

The following is a true story. I'm sorry to all those friends, acquaintances and other people who I've met along the way, who never made it into this book. I couldn't write everyone I've ever known in. And I'm sorry for all of those who made it in - who didn't want to be there! Some of the names have been changed.

CHAPTER 1

Destination London

With no idea what to expect next, I sat on the London-bound train as it pulled out of Worcester Foregate Street station. The Malvern Hills and Worcester Cathedral were close up now (in the city centre) and I stared at them, trying to take a permanent photograph, in my mind, to store and call upon whenever, just in case I never came back. It was the 22nd of March in 1982 and I was seventeen.

'I'm going to London,' I repeated to myself as the fear of the unknown crossed my mind and I felt a tremor in my hands. I tried to feel comforted by fooling myself I'd be back in a month if life didn't work out in the capital. I wondered how bad it would have to be for me to return to the city of Worcester. Coming back to a place where I'd been reduced to sleeping in a chip-shop doorway to shelter from the elements - seemed unlikely. The train was moving now and picking up speed.

I pressed my face up tightly against the train window, as children do, to try to grab the last few seconds of the picture perfect view, my favourite scene. In no time at all, Worcester was going out of sight but clear as anything in my mind's eye forever.

The man sitting opposite frowned at me, maybe unsure if I was an adult or a child by my appearance and behaviour. I tried to compose myself in a more dignified manner. I held my one-way child's ticket tightly in my right hand. What was left of my belongings rested in my luggage at my feet. One last look over my shoulder as the hills were starting to shrink and then the scene changed forever.

I used to think that if I cried hard enough that mum would somehow come back to me but that was the childish thinking of a fifteen-year-old. By seventeen I'd learned that death is the end and no amount of crying would ever resurrect her.

A mixture of despair, fear and excitement stayed with me for the majority of the two-and-a-half-hour limbo journey. Where did I belong now? The passing trees and buildings refused to give any answers. The old train tracks rattled and vibrated with a constant rhythm until intermittently we paused at different stations, names of which I no longer recognised.

'Where do I belong?' I whispered under my breath.

'Not here, not here, not here, not here' Replied the train tracks with perfectly timed clarity.

As time passed a new sense of hope overcame me - a new city, another day and a good friend that cared about me. Perhaps my life was about to change for the better. London was the place of dreams after all. Fate was about to throw me a new lifeline. I concluded that I was leaving misery behind, and my true destiny was about to commence.

The train soon approached its final stop at London Paddington and I prepared to disembark. As I looked through the dirty windows, I was amazed to see hundreds of people rushing around, all seemingly eager to get somewhere quickly with important issues to attend to. Still clutching my battered orange case and plastic carrier bags I exited the train with trepidation.

Since my friend Anna had told me to wait on my arrival platform, I found a bench and plonked myself down. My tired eyes darted about searching for her. But I couldn't see her and couldn't be sure she would even appear. My eyes repeatedly flicked from one face to another, automatically searching for one that I recognised. I was used to knowing so many people in my hometown and so naturally my nervous brain refused to rest my source of vision. I constantly searched for familiarity, a familiar face, someone, anyone! Fifteen minutes later and I suddenly felt exhausted and worried. 'Perhaps she's not coming to meet me.' My thoughts raced to consider a way to get back to my Worcester - without a return ticket but there was no turning back now.

The crowds, on the platform, thinned out and suddenly I noticed Anna rushing towards me with a huge smile on her freckled paleface and a darkskinned youth in tow. Relieved, I got up and walked towards them. Anna and I excitedly embraced one another and I was introduced to Geoff.

When Anna had lived in Worcester, she'd told me about Geoff. He'd been the cause of much trouble between her and her parents and part of the reason she'd been sent away to live in Worcester with her much older sister. I couldn't understand why her parents didn't like Geoff, he seemed so nice. 'Racism' she'd said. I didn't know anything about that. I'd never known anyone who wasn't white and English so it'd made no sense to me at all. All I knew was, Geoff seemed really genuine and friendly. I liked him instantly and wanted to touch his black curly hair.

I'd spoken to Geoff previously, of course, on the telephone and Anna had mentioned him so often that I felt we were already acquainted. His hair was fascinating, with its tiny black curls, that I couldn't resist touching it. I suppose that was inappropriate but he didn't seem to mind as he smiled at me with his kind face and perfectly white teeth.

We three seventeen-year-olds passed straight out of the train station and down the deepest escalators I'd ever encountered. The stench of diesel and sweat was overwhelming as we stood on a crowded platform and waited for the underground train. But the stench didn't seem to effect Anna or Geoff. This was a whole new adventure for me. My friends played a joke, telling me that I needed to make a request for the underground train to stop by putting my hand out. Like an out-of-town fool I did as they said and waved about frantically so the driver could see me. They laughed and so did I when I realised how stupid I must have looked. Thousands of unknown faces were all around us and I stayed close to my friends. I did not intend to get lost in this giant metropolis.

Since returning from Worcester, to live with her parents, Anna had enrolled on a typing course, in central London. It was sponsored by the Greater London Council and she received a payment, of thirty pounds per week, to attend. She'd become friends with a girl called Vicky who also attended this course. Both girls were living in unhappy circumstances and they'd come together and managed to scrape enough money to rent a kind of flat. Anna briefed me on the circumstances as we commuted across the capital.

We passed through Waterloo, so that I could meet Vicky and some of Anna's other collage acquaintances. Her friends found me fascinating as I had a strange accent. They gathered around, getting me to repeat words after them in my own way of talking. Every now and then one of them would check with Anna if I was 'for real.'

'Does she really talk like that or is she winding us up?' One of the boys asked.

'What's 'winding us up' mean?' I spoke with genuine confusion as I'd never heard that expression before. Everyone laughed and Anna assured them all that that was the way they talked back in Worcester.

After this, we said goodbye to Geoff and the others while Vicky, Anna and I took a train to an area called Gypsy Hill in south-east London. As I was out of money, Anna let me borrow some to pay for my fare.

Anna had been wholly unhappy living back with her parents in London. I'd not fully understood her anger or the situation when we'd been school friends in Worcester. Now Anna told the full story as Vicky and I listened intently and the rattly old train picked up speed. Something almost unbelievable had happened to Anna at the age of fourteen. She'd been raised in Battersea, south London, an already multicultural area and at school she became friends with children from a range of ethnic backgrounds. At fourteen she'd started to become attracted to boys, as is usual, but she tended to be more interested in the black boys. She was drawn to their music and their culture. Her parents were much older than was usual and perhaps stuck in their ways. Believing whites should stick with whites, they disapproved of Anna's interest in black company. And they had a misplaced hatred of her best-friend Geoff who was a good, kind boy from a decent, loving family.

Anna became more resentful towards her father especially and by way of rebelling, she deliberately enjoyed the attention of some older black boys and the wrong crowd. One night she made a big mistake. She willingly went along to, what she thought was, a party in a high-rise tower block. But she soon realised that she was the only girl. Four males held her captive all night, where something violent and disgusting was repeatedly done to her.

Disturbed by the trauma, Anna did not speak for a few days and her parents became irritated by her silence. Eventually she blurted out the whole awful story, of her ordeal. But instead of comforting her, Anna's parents blamed her for the incident. She was dragged to the police station to undergo a medical but as several days had passed, since the attack, all evidence was gone.

There may have been an atmosphere of institutional racism in the overwhelmingly white force at that time. The police somehow picked up on the fact that Anna preferred the company of the black crowd by the way she dressed and they decided to also blame her for what had happened.

She was either a liar, as the attack never happened, or worse - it was consensual. The obscene and descriptive words, used against a fourteen-year-old, were shocking to say the very least. She left the station with the officers' vicious words ringing in her ears. Worse still, the police officers' assumption only confirmed her parent's preconceptions. None of the perpetrators were ever convicted or even questioned about the attack. Anna's label of 'slag' was the least offensive of the constabulary's vocabulary.

Anna's parents decided that the best course of action was to get their fourteen-year-old daughter away from London. She was separated from all of her friends, including Geoff. She was banished to live in Worcester with her much older, married sister. The agreement was that she would live there for her last two years of schooling. Except for having me as her friend, she was lost and miserable there. She was a fish out of water and could not wait to return to London.

As school was done with us at the age of sixteen, Anna returned to London. There, she commenced the typing course where she met and became friends with Vicky. And Vicky's story was no better.

On first meeting Vicky, you'd think she had it all. Not only was she very attractive with her short dark hair, creamy white skin and huge brown eyes but she was highly intelligent, even bordering on genius. But she did not have it all. She'd never known her Father and was raised in abject poverty, although lovingly, by her mother alone. Mother and daughter regularly moved from one rented flat to another, around south east London. Although their lives were difficult, Vicky's mother dedicated herself to Vicky's education and evenings were spent in reading and intellectual discussion. They were extremely close.

Vicky only reached the age of eleven when her mother died suddenly from a massive asthma attack. There were no available relatives coming forward to claim Vicky and so with an eleven-year-old, the Social Services were immediately and directly involved. (An eleven-year-old in London being much easier to rehome than I'd been as a teenager in Worcester.) She was immediately placed into foster-care.

As Vicky's body started to develop her foster Father showed inappropriate affection towards her. For some time, she misunderstood and believed his 'cuddles' to be that of a loving-father. When the penny-dropped she was repulsed but there was nowhere to go. At the age of fifteen she moved out. She went to stay with an eighteen-year-old boyfriend who she believed herself to be in love with at the time. But after a few short weeks the boyfriend became jealous and aggressive and Vicky changed her mind about living with him and his mother. She was desperate to escape while she too was attending the typing course where she'd met Anna.

CHAPTER 2

Accommodation

All three of us had come through some terrible storms. Perhaps we were early casualties of a failing society. I'd heard that the war years of the 1940's had brought the English solidarity and strengthened community. This had lead into the fifties where there continued to be strict rules of English society built on religious standards of behaviour. People went to church on Sundays and television wasn't mainstream yet. Families had conversation and made their own entertainment which served to strengthen their bonds. The rules dictated 'no sex before marriage' and if it did happen and a girl got pregnant, a shot-gun wedding would swiftly ensue. Society would insist on it. When the parents got old, their children naturally cared for them. Communities and religious leaders had always encouraged families to stay close to each other. Then the 1960s saw a technology boom and the television set became mainstream to the dismay of pious Christian folk. 'It's the work of the devil!' they cried. But no one was listening as people wanted a telly.

The Swinging-Sixties also saw the development of the birth control pill and women's liberation was born instead of many children. Females could be 'just like men' now as they too could enjoy sex, recreationally. By the seventies sexual promiscuity was subtly encouraged via the television that now occupied almost all living rooms. Virginity at the point of marriage was now seen as old-fashioned and 'free-love' was the motto of the day. Controlling levels of off-spring was the new modern phenomenon. Sexual liberation was also subtly encouraged (and eventually overtly encouraged) via the mainstream television and this coincided with mass-infidelity. There was a massive drop in church attendance as the majority watched and listened to the preaching of the British Broadcasting Company, rather than the old-fashioned vicar.

Instead of staying close to family, newly married couples such as my parents and Anna's parents, felt the freedom to move away from their kin in search of better pay and independance. Vicky's Mum had been unmarried, a liberated woman, who'd gone off by herself to have her baby girl. I guess it may have seemed like a good idea at the time but when the shit hit the fan, well, there was just no backup plan.

There was no extended family or community

around to keep an eye on Anna and to explain to her the error of her ways. The mixture of cultures in her area only further muddled-up and confused society's rules. There was no relative to care for Vicky once her Mum had died. And I'd had so little contact with my extended family that they felt it easier to turn their backs on me after my immediate family's rejection. There was no longer real 'community' as such and the adults, in general, cared less and less about God's judgement these days. The idea of me asking the church for help was so far removed that it never even crossed my mind.

We casualties were an early symptom of the flaws in the new modern system. The state was beginning to implement the picking up of the pieces from the inevitable family breakdowns. But the new system was not tried and tested and in years to come the authorities would become overwhelmed with the fallout.

The 1980's were a financially prosperous decade and greed was no longer a sin. More and more families separated themselves from their kin in pursuit of money and their dreams, not foreseeing their nightmares if the waters were to become choppy. In the near future thousands of lonely, elderly people would struggle to fend for themselves or have their lifesavings spent on their own personal care from unrelated, paid-assistants. This sickness was close on the horizon but yet to be fully realised. We three girls were yet to realise ourselves; we were far too busy trying to keep our heads above water to understand that the system, for the majority, was on the verge of falling apart too.

Obesity and depression were unused words in the fifties - when they started to regularly appear in the eighties, people were at a loss to understand. 'We must educate the masses on what to eat, 'the 'experts' would insist, 'for they know not what they do.' They could not comprehend that the great demise of our society, coupled with big food giants' radical campaigns to sell cheap-to-produce plastic foods, through television advertising, were responsible.

I'd had no support system in back up and neither did Vicky. Anna's backup had forced her away from everything she knew and held dear. Her banishment to Worcester had therefore been taken as a punishment. Now we three found ourselves together in the dog-eat-dog capital of London. We just didn't understand anything yet. We were too busy licking our wounds.

Anna and Vicky had somehow managed to rent a double room in a terraced house. A teaching assistant named Ben, from their college, owned a small place in Gypsy hill, south London. He'd needed some extra money, so he'd offered for the girls to have his upstairs room at a minimal price. It was a mutually beneficial arrangement or so it seemed at first. But the awkwardness of sharing the kitchen and bathroom with teaching-assistant-Ben soon became apparent and within a matter of weeks the atmosphere turned sour. Vicky and Anna were inept at budgeting and things only got much worse as they missed a rental payment. As the atmosphere turned nasty, the girls stopped paying rent altogether and Ben felt forced to initiate legal papers to evict them. By the time I arrived at the property the 'notice to quit' had already been served on them and there were only three weeks left before we would all be evicted. I'd known this before I arrived in London but with no other options for a roof over my head, three weeks was better than nothing at all.

On arrival, at the house, I immediately met Ben. I could see he felt awkward. I tried to reassure him, with my polite manner, that I would be no trouble at all, if only I could stay. He seemed relieved and resigned to accommodate me providing we all left on the official day of eviction.

Anna showed me the upstairs room and I noticed it was unfurnished with just a double mattress on the floor. There were no wardrobes or cupboards, just four cold and empty walls. Vicky's clothes were piled up in one corner and Anna's clothes were in a heap in another. I placed my orange case and plastic carrier bags down on the floor. There were no curtains or any other home comforts but there was central-heating and a warmth from my friends that was reassuring.

I was to sleep in the middle of the double mattress in-between the two girls. The three of us lost-souls huddled up together like vagabonds. Anna and Vicky cuddled me all night, so desperate were they to be mothered. It was the most wanted and needed I'd felt in a long while.

Over the next week, Anna and Vicky took me to the benefits office and arranged for my unemployment claim to be moved from Worcester to the area we were in, in south-east London. As we'd be leaving Ben's house soon, I could not give it as my permanent address. So, I was listed as a 'no fixed abode claimant.' A few days later I went back to the benefits office and collected my giro-cheque from the 'special section' - along with the other strays and homeless people. By now the amount in London was £16 per week. I cashed my giro at a post office and paid out the money that I owed to my two friends for trains, busses, the launderette and food.

I guessed I'd lost some weight but I gave this notion little thought. Our daily consumption consisted of the occasional shop-bought sandwich and a cream cake or a bag of chips. These items may have been calorific but for a whole day they were a small amount and almost totally devoid of vitamins and minerals. I just didn't think about what I should or shouldn't be consuming. I was unmothered. A child in the body of an adolescent nearing womanhood. We three were unmothered. Sandwiches, chips and cakes were the extent of our daily consumption, except for our evening trips to the local public house - where we topped up our calories with alcohol.

In the pub, we would buy ourselves a drink just to sit somewhere nice. Usually, we'd only have to pay out for one or two drinks and then we generally received alcohol from interested males. Us being underage didn't seem to concern anyone or perhaps no one realised. We may have passed for adults by this time and no one ever asked our ages or seemed to care.

As the deadline approached for our eviction date, we turned to these men in the public house for any ideas on where we could live. We were in a difficult position; landlords didn't want 17-year-old tenants and three was an awkward number. And we had no references and no deposit money.

By the evening, before the day of our eviction, one of these young men came up with an immediate plan of action. He was a skinhead (a subculture of youths) who was living in a local squat, and we were welcome to move in with him and his acquaintances.

Anna decided against the option of squatting with a gang of unknown youths. She went begrudgingly back for a temporary stay closer to central London, with her parents in nearby Battersea. Vicky would still see Anna at her collage. And I had every intention of keeping in touch with Anna but I guess the road to hell is paved with good intentions. Vicky and I had no such parents and in the absence of any other option we took up the offer of the squat.

CHAPTER 3

Squatters

On eviction day, a whole team of skinheads turned up to assist Vicky and I with our move. We didn't have much stuff so our items were transported easily on foot. We didn't know where we were going but we'd been informed that it was within the local area.

We followed the convoy of skinheads, through a park until we came to several rows of streets filled with decrepit Victorian terrace houses. These were old and failing buildings that, from the outside, seemed uninhabited. Apparently, these derelict properties were waiting to be demolished and all the inhabitants had been rehomed or removed in one way or another. As the homeowners and tenants moved out, some of the houses had been taken by squatters. Some of these squatters were desperate types who'd fallen on hard-times for one reason or another. Some were drug-addicts but I was so naïve and innocent that I hadn't realised at the time. Others were ordinary people who just needed to shelter from the cold.

The mid-terrace house, that we were taken to, was already inhabited by eight skinheads. The electricity was still connected or perhaps illegally reconnected and there was running water available. The wooden floor-boards were still in reasonably good condition but there was an immediate sense of emptiness and an echo from the lack of carpets, furniture and fittings. Mattresses could be seen on the floors of the rooms that had their doors ajar. Territories had already been claimed and the youths had made their sections of the house their own, as best they could.

The youths, who were all in their early twenties, carried our belongings up to the only available room which was the attic. There were two single mattresses, in there, already prepared for us. We laid our things out and tried to make ourselves comfortable as best we could.

The guys were friendly enough and hospitable as much as they were able, having nothing much to offer. One of them had come across some tinned dog-food, possibly stolen. He'd helped himself to some free salt sachets from the local burger-bar and he bashed open one of the tins and sprinkled a little salt onto the sloppy dog meat. With a plastic spoon he politely offered for me to eat first insisting it really tasted ok with the salt. I recoiled by reflex and then quickly recomposed myself and then politely refused. He smiled and said I was to have some later-on if or when I was very hungry.

Dog-eat-dog, stray dogs, dogs and bitches. Human's eating dog food to survive. We were not far from the famous Battersea dog's home in more ways than one. But the dog's home dogs were not eating stolen meat and they had bowels to eat from. Dogs had a purpose in life - to complete someone's happy home one day. If that day never came they would eventually be destroyed. We had little purpose in life and would destroy ourselves one way or another if we didn't soon find one.

Two or three more of our new friends had come to chat with us in the attic and they had something to smoke with them. Cannabis smoking was something I'd never witnessed before. I was not a smoker but as the joint was passed around from person to person, Vicky was trying it and then, with her encouragement, I did too. I didn't like the feeling of dizziness that came over me, I lay down on one of the mattresses and pulled my jacket across my cold legs. Vicky followed suit. It may have been an hour later or maybe three, we'd lost track of time but we woke to find our whole attic room full of skinheads crashed-out around us. I suddenly felt very vulnerable and as I glanced over at Vicky, I could see she felt the same. We spent the rest of the dark hours awake and guarded. We watched the boys with their little packets of green leaves and other paraphernalia. They would periodically wake up, skin up, then go into some kind of trace and then sleep again. I was thinking we needed to get out of this place and by Vicky's expression I could see she was thinking the same.

'We ain't staying ere' Vicky side-whispered with her hand over her mouth, in an attempt to funnel the sound purely in my direction.

'Where we gonna go?' I whispered back to her. She knew her way around London and she was my only hope.

'I dunno' She said, 'but we ain't staying ere'

How would we leave and where would we go? We didn't want to offend anyone. These skinheads had been good to us in their own way. They had next to nothing of material value in this life but they'd shared what little they had. They'd gone to the trouble of locating a couple of old mattresses; they'd offered their dog food and shared their weed. None of them had tried their luck with us but we didn't want to wait around for that to happen. We needed to get out, get out quickly and with as little fuss as possible. Luckily, after several hours, the boys either left the attic to return to their own rooms or were fully crashed-out, stoned, on the attic floor. We hastily packed up our bags and tiptoed out of the house as the new day dawned. I felt sorry and guilty to sneak out like that, they'd done us no harm.

It's almost impossible to describe the feelings of despair I felt as we walked about on that cold April morning. Lost, disorientated, lonely, desperate, exhausted, terrified, depressed, hopeless, a longing to be loved and to mean something to someone - none of these words or sentences can really do it justice. Walking around and not knowing where you will sleep at night whilst carrying everything you own (which was nothing of material value) is just an indescribable concoction of emotion.

At this point, I'd been living in London for almost a month. It was at this point that I seriously toyed with the idea of buying a train ticket back to Worcester where, at least, I knew I was confident of knowing my way around. But after two years of moving from place to place there, that just seemed pointless and a waste of time, effort and money.

Anyway, I guessed I now meant something to Vicky. We definitely leaned on each other and supported one another but I always needed her more than she needed me. I was the out-of-towner and I was reliant on her not purely as my only friend but also to navigate me around this unknown city. She knew her way around this side of London, she was street-wise. Although she was clearly damaged by her childhood years, she wasn't in the same weak state of bereavement and despair that I was in. I relied on Vicky for everything from navigation and decision making to counselling in attempt to boost my emotional strength.

As we peered through the cracks in some of the condemned buildings around us, we could see that many of them had already been taken by squatters. Those houses that hadn't gone already, hadn't gone for good reason - such as they were too dangerous to enter.

We approached a house that appeared to be empty and I opened up the letter-box to try to peer in. It was difficult to see anything inside as all the windows were boarded up ready for demolition and there was very little light available for my eyes to register information. Suddenly the door opened and we shot back with a start! We cowed a little with fear but the face that greeted us appeared kind as he smiled. As a guess I would say he was in his late twenties, a dark haired, bearded man of medium stature. We apologised profusely and turned to walk away. To our surprise the man started to make polite conversation with us. He started explaining that his name was Bobby and how he and his friend Pete had only just recently taken the house themselves. We explained that we were desperate for a place to stay and that we had obviously intended to take this place for ourselves.

As we stood on the doorstep, like two pathetic and bedraggled rag-dolls, Bobby called up the stairs to his friend Pete, who immediately made his way down to meet us. Pete also had a brown beard but it was much bushier, he seemed the older of the two. He was rather less approachable although he listened intently as we continued on with the story of our predicament. Bobby looked tenderly at Pete and Pete nodded back sympathetically. Out of the blue, Bobby suggested we could stay in the house with the two of them, and Pete did not hesitate with his agreement. These two men had kindly offered for us to join them. They proposed that they would live upstairs and we down.

We had little choice but to trust these two un-known characters, just as we'd done with the skinheads before them. We placed our belongings in the downstairs of the house and introduced ourselves properly to our new house-mates. The younger, Bobby, was a chatty type while Pete was far more reserved in nature. They both seemed friendly though and they gave us a key to the new lock that Pete had recently fitted on the front door. Bobby advised that we should immediately go out and find throw-away mattresses for ourselves, out on the surrounding streets.

We searched around the local rows of condemned terrace houses and then, as we continued on, we found ourselves in a normal kind of area. An area with regular, well maintained terrace houses. Looking at the crispy white net-curtains of nor-mality, I felt sharp green with envy. How lucky these people were to have the comfort of families and a warm place to stay. My juvenile thinking made me assume that they all possessed the con-tentment that was missing from my life. I couldn't imagine that they could have their own miseries, not while they had warms homes with white nets! Did they appreciate it, did they realise the riches they possessed?

Vicky and I discussed incessantly, the pros and cons of sleeping on someone else's throw-away mattress in comparison to the other option of sleeping on a hard wooden floor with no mattress at all. This would not only be very uncomfortable it may also have been dangerously cold. We agreed that a throw-away mattress was our best option. We also discussed my main concern, I was afraid about moving in with these two men who we did not know at all. Although they appeared to be kind enough and friendly, it still seemed very risky but what choice did we have?

Vicky comforted me by saying that Bobby and Pete were obviously 'gay' but I didn't know if this was true. I had heard about such things but I'd never actually met a gay person in real life as far as I knew. How Vicky instinctively knew this I could not work out but she said it was obvious and I was naive not to see it. But I didn't really know what I was looking for or what the signs were.

'Oh, you make me laugh,' Vicky said. She was clearly amused as she continued 'Where ave you come from - you're Such a farmer!'

Vicky shook her head in disbelief and we both bust out laughing. I wasn't sure if she was just trying to put my mind at rest by convincing me of Bobby and Pete's lack of sexual interest in us. Or if they were truly in love and only attracted to each other as Vicky had insisted. Vicky was adamant that the two men had zero attraction towards us girls or females in general. I certainly had no intention of asking the two men about their desires or their relationship. I didn't want to put my foot in it and I didn't want to offend anyone.

We circulated in the circumference of around a mile from the squats and then made our way back through in the direction of our basecamp. We had little chance of finding any mattresses at all in this area, let alone anything half decent. Still searching, we knew that anything usable would have most likely been already taken by other squatters. It seemed ironic that the skinheads had gone to the trouble of locating two reasonably clean mattresses for us (probably the last two for miles around) and now they were placed on an attic floor, unused. Perhaps we could go back to the skinheads and ask for the mattresses? No, that didn't seem right at all. There were rules in this dog-eat-dog squatting society, I'd worked that out already. And we'd broken the rules by disrespecting the skinheads' hospitality. We already dreaded bumping into them, so actually knocking on their door and having the nerve to ask for mattresses, was out of the question.

Eventually as the daylight began to fade, we managed to secure a baby cot-mattress that'd been thrown into the bushes. It was filthy-dirty but would have to do. At least it would be better than sleeping on the floor-boards, which was our only other choice by this point.

Our latest squat was less habitable than the skinheads' house. The broken windows were totally boarded up, allowing just a few trickles of sunlight to filter through during the daylight hours. Several of the wooden floor-boards were broken, making it already treacherous to walk across what would have been the original living-room floor. There was no running water which meant no working toilet or washing facilities and the electricity wiring had been permanently disconnected and partially removed. Ceased out. The back of the house was not to be ventured into at all. Bobby said we could injure ourselves out there so best avoid it entirely.

Still on the plus side, our housemates seemed really nice and caring and at least it was better than sleeping on a card box out on the street somewhere. For young females, that would be a danger akin to suicidal.

Some of the floorboards were rotting and dangerously weak. But we found a corner in the original living-room, that looked like it would be able to cope with the weight of the baby mattress and our tiny bodies. Then we tried to make ourselves comfortable.

We went out and bought ourselves a bag of chips to share and later we went to the nearby public house and got ourselves a drink. We took it in turns to go the empty ladies-toilets to try to have a strip-wash as best we could. With no towel available I managed with the one that was in the ladies for general use and I had my toothbrush and paste with me to give my teeth a good clean. Strangely, no matter what my circumstances, I usually managed to clean my teeth. Maybe it was a ritual that kept me connected to what it meant to be human. I've no idea, it was just something I generally insisted on getting done. A little bit like an obsession that had developed recently. Just since arriving at the squat-life.

As I came back to my drink, Vicky went off to clean herself and we both felt a lot better for it. By the time we'd finished the beverages we'd purchased, we'd managed to attract the attention of some young builders who were currently regulars at this establishment. They were in the demolition business, and you can easily guess what they were in the process of demolishing. We spent the rest of the evening chatting and receiving drinks which they purchased for us. As closing time approached we said goodbye to our new friends. We knew we would see them again, as this public house was now the place of our toilet and washing facilities.

Vicky and I were both tipsy as we tried to locate the house that we were staying in. But the street lights were on and we found the building without too much difficulty. I had the key in my pocket and so I unlocked the door and stepped into the corridor. It was pitch black and I realised that we'd made a mistake. We should've taken some matches out with us so as to be able to see on our return. If we could just manage to get to the baby mattress, we would be ok but before I knew it, I'd gone straight through a broken floor-board and I could feel the blood trickling down my leg.

'Ouch!' I squealed in pain and frustration.

'You ok Jen?' Vicky called out with obvious concern.

'Stop, don't move, try and keep over to the edges, I mean straddle your legs to the sides' I said.

'What, oh ok.' Vicky couldn't see me; she could only hear me telling her where she should and should not try to step. It was not so easy for her to take instructions in the darkness.

Eventually, with my left hand, I found the living room door and pushed it open. A crack in the boarded-up broken windows allowed a trickle of light in from the streetlights outside and by now my eyes had adjusted a little. Vicky and I lay down together on the baby mattress. We squashed up together fully dressed. It was so cold so we hugged each other all night.

The next morning, Vicky's little alarm clock had

woken her up and now she was out at typing college in central London. I woke up cold and went straight upstairs. I told Bobby about how I'd fallen through the broken floor boards. We had to try and see the funny side of it and we smiled and then laughed about it. Then he gave me a box of matches, two candles and a sticky-plaster for my leg. I went back to our area of the house and stuck the plaster onto the dried blood near my knee. Before I forgot, I quickly put the box of matches into one jacket pocket and one of the candles into the other pocket.

It was so cold and the temperature didn't seem to improve throughout the day. Hardly any of the April sunlight could pierce its way through the boards on the broken windows and so I waited in near darkness. I sat on the baby mattress and looked at the fireplace. I found a piece of paper and with the matches I lit it up and placed it in the fireplace. The warmth on my hands felt lovely if only for a few seconds.

I went out on the street and found an old newspaper blowing about like a silent tumble-weed. Back in the house I started to pull apart the pages. I rolled them into balls and then proceeded to light them one by one. Watching all the colours flashing up in front of me for a minute or two, I felt some warmth on my face. Then it was cold again, so cold that my hands were itching. I rocked myself back and forth.

Soon enough Vicky was back and we went out together to the chemist. We needed some female necessities. We also purchased some fizzy-drinks and a cream-cake each. We ate the cakes up with gusto, within seconds, on the walk back to the house. The sun was on its way down by now but still light enough to manoeuvre without the risk of falling inside the house. We'd forgotten to get more candles and matches while out and we didn't want to use the last candle if not absolutely necessary. Anyway, we were starting to memorise where we could and could not stand safely. The safest technique was to straddle and shuffle in the corridor. The edges near the old skirting-boards seemed the strongest part of the flooring and also guided us to the old living-room door on the left. From there on we could make it to the baby-mattress safely.

We sat and chatted for a while and within a few minutes we became almost unbearably cold. There were a couple of pieces of broken wooden floorboard, further down the corridor towards the back of the house. I'd memorised where they were and I went and carefully lifted a couple of pieces into the living room. I shoved a chunk into the fire-place and I called out to Pete to come and see if he could make up a fire for us. Pete was good with stuff like that and within minutes he'd managed to get a roaring fire going.

Bobby and Pete stayed downstairs and chatted with us for a while. Bobby had a few food items with him for us to share, some cheese and whole tomatoes. With a tiny pen-knife he chopped up the tomatoes and sprinkled a pinch of salt on a half that he handed over to me. I was hungry and nothing could have tasted more delicious. He was very concerned, insisting we two girls needed to take better care of ourselves.

After Bobby and Pete left our room, Vicky and I huddled over the fire, the orange light brightly colouring our young faces. We chatted for a while and discussed our lives, funny events, stupid stories and all the traumas we'd suffered. I was getting on well with my new best friend. She said I was so funny that I should be a stand-up comedienne! Really, I had no clue as to why I could often see the amusing side of things in life. Generally, of late, I was either laughing hysterically or crying and nothing much else was to be found in between. But perhaps Vicky was just being nice by trying to boost my confidence and couldn't find much else to say other than saying I was so funny. We often tried to boost each other up after that.

Options for our futures were not many. At seventeen, neither one of us would be able to register for council accommodation but there was hope. Vicky was officially registered as an orphan and even though she'd walked out on her foster family, she'd been shrewd enough to remain on the social services 'in-Care' books. Of course, she'd never told her social worker of the real reason why she'd left her foster parents. She'd always been too ashamed and embarrassed to repeat the story and she'd always blamed herself. But anyway, being on the books of the social services in London meant that she was likely to get a council flat as soon as she reached eighteen.

It was the light at the end of the tunnel and we chatted and dreamed about how we would decorate and furnish the flat, which could be a home for the both of us. We decided and agreed that one of the rooms would be really modern and another would be an old style, like a stately home or a palace. I could visualise it clearly in my mind's eye and fantasied about it. We smiled and felt happy at the thought of it. We just needed to survive the next six months until Vicky would turn eighteen. Then, we would be saved.

In the meantime we didn't intend on staying in the squats. We needed to try to rent a flat privately. We knew this was not going to be easy in our position. Landlords didn't generally take on minors as tenants and to add to that we had no jobs, no deposit and we couldn't afford much rent. Vicky only had her £30 a week allowance from the college course and I had the small amount of £16 from benefits, which was not going to impress anyone. I probably could have gotten help with rental payments from the social but I just didn't know it at this time. My monthly allowance, from my mother's will, was hardly worth mentioning and on top of that, competition for cheap housing was rife.

CHAPTER 4

Crystal Palace

We continued our lives at the squat with Bobby and Pete and we continued to go the public house to try to scrub ourselves and clean our teeth. Our finger nails were usually black from the soot of the open fire and there was nowhere to wash our hair.

We lived in the aptly named Gypsy hill area which was not too far from the Crystal Palace national sports centre. One day the street-wise Vicky came up with a great idea. We would take our washing things and sneak into the sports centre for a hot shower! This would turn out to be easier said than done.

We walked through the main entrance of the sports centre with confidence as if we had a keep-fit class or tennis lesson to attend. But we were stopped in our tracks at reception by an overzealous, female employee. We left the building and wandered around the vast green park and grounds that had once housed the old Crystal Palace (before it burned down to the ground) and now housed the famous sports centre. We sat down on a park-bench and considered a second attempt. We racked our brains to come up with an idea or a story to get us through the main entrance of the sports centre. Then out of the blue it hit me that we should try to find another entrance or exit to the sports centre so as to bypass the receptionist.

We wandered around the huge building and located a rear exit but it was impossible to pull the door open from the outside. I shook it again and again in frustration. We really needed to take a shower and we had been so looking forward to it. Then all of a sudden the door was flung open from the inside by an angry looking, huge, black security guard.

We were afraid and apologised profusely. The angry security guard demanded we explain ourselves as to why we were attempting to get in through the rear exit doors of the sports centre. Well, I couldn't come up with a good enough story and I just looked at Vicky in defeat. With nothing to lose and out of complete desperation, Vicky commenced to tell him the truth the whole truth and nothing but the truth. Then we both explained that we lived in a squat without water, gas or electricity and were absolutely desperate for a shower! It was obvious that our story was true as we were blurting it out together with no chance to confer. To our amazement, the security guard took pity on us and opened the back doors wide for us to come through. He pointed us in the direction of the female changing rooms and told us where we could locate him when we were finished.

It was the best shower of my life. We'd purchased a cheap bottle of shampoo on our way to the centre and now we were under the steaming hot water with the power shower jets forcing their way down on our anguished, filthy bodies. We didn't want to come out of there and by the time we did we must have been in there for an hour or more.

As agreed, when we left the changing rooms, we went to find the security guard. As he saw us he walked forward and spoke in a lowered tone so as no one else could overhear. He inquired as to our enjoyment of the facilities and we responded with a great deal of enthusiasm. Then to our disbelief he offered for us to take a shower at the centre as and whenever we wanted. As long as he was on duty, if he heard us tap on the same rear exit, he would open the door and let us in. After informing us of his days and hours of on and off duties, we thanked him a thousand times and even kissed him on his cheeks when no one was looking. The sports centre was a bit of a trek from the squats and although we intended to take him up on his kind offer, we never did.

During the week, Vicky was out at college and I would spend my days alone in the squat. I tried to lay and sleep on the baby mattress for as long as I could in the mornings but without Vicky's body heat, I felt very cold very soon after she'd left for the day. Bobby had kindly given us a blanket and we would sleep in almost as many clothes as we owned. But even though we were now in May, summer had still not really arrived. And with no heating and next to no sunlight being able to reach through the boarded, broken windows, the temperature inside the old living room still felt extremely cold.

I sat up on the mattress and leaned against the cold, brick wall. I tried to shove my hands into my jeans pockets to warm them a little. I looked up at a thin stream of sunlight that was pushing its way through the cracks in the boarded-up window and wondered when these houses would be raised to the ground. The builders had already started with a wrecking-ball on the next street so we knew we didn't have long. I looked over at Vicky's belongings. She didn't have much stuff. Then this thought popped into my head. 'What would I do if she didn't come back?'

I felt a little hungry so I put my shoes on and walked to the bakery. I didn't want to explore too far from the squats as I could easily get lost. Two or three streets away to the bakery and I was about as far as I would venture alone. I bought myself a sandwich and ate it hurriedly on my way back to the squat. I needed the toilet now and luckily the public house was open. I could nip in there as the Ladies' toilets were directly inside the main entrance on the right, (Men on the left.) This meant I could use the facilities without having to purchase a drink from the bar and without being seen by the bar staff. That was a stroke of luck. While I was in there I washed my face. I always had my tooth brush and paste in one pocket and a candle and a box of matches in the other pocket. Just a quick wash now and I would come back later with Vicky 'if she came back.' 'When she came back!' Why did I say if she came back? Why was I worrying that she might not come back?

Because she was all I had!

Later in the afternoon Vicky was back with me and we went for a walk to see how the demolitions were going. We bumped into an older guy we recognized from the public house and it turned out he was living in one of the squats too. He invited us in for a smoke and we accepted. Again, I didn't really enjoy the feeling that came over me and I just felt groggy and wanted to sleep. But I stayed awake as a few of his friends joined us. The joints kept being rolled up and passed around, they just kept coming.

We were totally stoned when we left the other squat. Luckily, I had the candle and matches to light up our way into our place. We both needed the toilet now. It was too late to walk up to the public house as it was way past closing time. There was a toilet at the back of the house but we were not to use it. There was danger all around with rubble and broken glass everywhere. The broken toilet had no water to flush it and it was blocked with rubble and smelt fowl. Inside and outside the house, everything had been ripped out by builders, as an attempt to discourage the nuisance of people like us. Best option was for us to go and relieve ourselves in the dark and hazardous back yard.

With the lit candle, we carefully negotiated our way through the dangerous rear section of the house. This was more treacherous than the front as more floor-boards were missing and piles of rubble littered the place. As a consequence, we'd not learned our way around and didn't know which areas were safe and unsafe to stand on. In the dark I felt scared - really scared.

I was holding the candle and Vicky was starting to giggle behind me. I don't know why, maybe the effect of the cannabis was making her find this situation so amusing. Maybe she was laughing at me? She always said I was so funny. I pretended to laugh too and before I knew it, we were both laughing hysterically. The tragic, hysterical comedy of the situation combined with the effects of the cannabis seemed to confuse something in my head. I suddenly realised that I wouldn't be able to clean my teeth this night and soon enough the comedic situation was looking like a disaster. My laughter rapidly switched to uncontrollable gibbering. And my dry eyes flowed with tears. Then I could hear in Vicky's voice that she was upset too. What the hell were we going to do - not just about the imminent toilet situation but our hopeless lives in general.

The back-yard was surrounded by other deserted and overgrown back yards. We did what we had to do by the light of the moon. Then I picked up the candle from just inside the building and we carefully made our way back to the baby mattress.

We talked for a while and I ended up crying over the stupidest thing in the world. I wanted to clean my teeth and I couldn't. Vicky calmed me down by talking to me and then explaining how to just put a spot of toothpaste behind my front teeth. She said, that way the taste of the paste goes straight to your brain and you can convince yourself everything's ok. It didn't really work but I managed to calm down about it for Vicky's sake and before long we slept. Vicky said I'd disturbed her several times by shouting out in my sleep. I had a vague recollection of it. I knew I'd been sleep-thrashing for quite a while by now.

The light at the end of the tunnel was that Vicky's social worker would help her to get a council flat when she got to be eighteen. We fantasized about how we would furnish it. We imagined something like the interior of a palace with luxurious furniture and fittings. We would have a bathroom in the flat and we both longed to take a bath.

I'd heard that one of the squats had a bath with hot running water! Apparently, the occupier of that squat was quite agreeable and might let me take a bath if I asked nicely. So, while Vicky was at college one day, I got the guy that I knew from the public house to introduce me to the one with the bath.

The one with the bath was a good-looking man of about twenty-five, named Paul. He was a classically tall, dark and handsome individual. And his house was not like a squat at all. There were carpets and furniture. There was even a television and cooking facilities. It was unbelievable really. You would never have thought it a squat. Paul invited me in then made me a cup of tea and gave me a biscuit. We sat on the bed and watched television. I hadn't watched television for several months and therefore felt fully entertained.

We chatted and he told me all about himself. He had a job as one of the managers of the McDonald's burger bar in the nearby Crystal Palace area. He had a girlfriend who normally lived with him but she was now away in hospital on a pre-natal ward. I guess there was some connection between her being pregnant and them having more amenities in their house. Or perhaps Paul and his girlfriend had moved in quickly and got there before the builders came to wreck the house initially. You'd have to be heartless to smash up such a decent place especially while a pregnant woman resided there. They were awaiting their first child and fully expected to be allocated a council home as soon as the baby was born.

I enjoyed a restful bath and as I'd completely forgotten to bring the only towel I had, which was a hand towel that Bobby had given to me, Paul lent me a bath towel. This was luxury. After bathing and dressing myself, Paul and I sat on the bed again as there was no sitting room or settee. Paul said he might be able to get me a job in his burger bar and I should come back again and have another bath the next day and then we could discuss it.

I liked Paul. He was an attractive young man and I enjoyed being in the comforts of his squat-home. In the kingdom of the blind the one-eyed man is king, and in the realm of the squats the house with carpets and furniture is luxurious. That house is a palace and that squatter - the King.

'Ya know there is another kind of work that you and Vicky could do, something that pays a whole lot better than flipping burgers?' Paul announced on my second visit, 'This is London and two pretty girls like you two could make loads of money, easy. You're both sitting on a fortune.'

'Really? What can we do?' I asked with childlike enthusiasm.

Paul lent towards me and put his mouth on top of mine.

I had next to nothing in this world; my nearest

and dearest relatives had disowned me and I was lost in a huge city of unknown faces. My spirit was low as my physical attractiveness was reaching its peak. I was becoming an easy combination for young men who couldn't help themselves. My desire to be cared for and loved, placed me in a precarious position. Added to this I didn't understand men at all, having been raised in an all-female family with an absent Father. I was the metaphorical lamb to the slaughter. Desperate for love and attention, a sheep in sheep's clothing.

'Wait a minute' I pulled myself away from Paul, 'Are you suggesting we become prostitutes?'

'Look, I can get you a job at my place, that's not a problem and it's up to you, I'm just saying, you can work day and night for a crap wage or you could have an easy life, a comfortable life, doing next to nothing, just think about it, I know people, I can help you,' He spoke sincerely.

I had to take Paul's proposition seriously. I liked him, I kind-of trusted him, he seemed to have our best interests at heart and he seemed sensible and mature. We were in a terrible position, living in squats with little hope. Even if I worked day and night in McDonalds, it was unlikely we'd ever be able to afford to rent a flat. And these squat-houses would be demolished soon and then what?

What Paul had suggested might be 'easy money' but what would I have left if I sold my soul to the devil. At least Paul was open and honest about his idea, while the devil usually comes in deception and disguise.

Money was essential if Vicky and I were to escape the hovel we frequented as our current home. So the next day I went to enjoy another bath and visit Paul. He was very happy as his baby boy had been born during the night. They would call the baby Kris, he'd said, Kris with a K and only one S. Well, that seemed very modern.

We had a cup of tea and I stayed with Paul for a while. He'd arranged for me to have an interview with the store manager at the burger bar the very next day. I could take a bath and scrub the ash, from the open fire, out of my nails in the morning, before the interview. That would be my last bath there as the girlfriend and baby Kris were coming home soon. Paul assured me I would get the job at the burger-bar as long as I didn't have filthy finger nails.

Luckily Paul had put a good word in and after a very quick and relaxed 'interview' the manager offered for me to start working the very next day. He explained that the hours would be on a shift basis and I confirmed that this would not be a problem. I didn't know what to expect from this employment but I was happy to have it and Vicky and I dared to think that we might be able to rent a flat with my wage and her college allowance combined together. I didn't want to resort to vice to drag myself out of the underground world of squats and drugs but I had to admit to myself that it was a definite possibility.

CHAPTER 5

Feral

By the beginning of June, things were looking up. I was starting to enjoy my new job even though the hours were all over the place and the work was no picnic. Summer had arrived and at last I was making friends. My first pay packet was due and Vicky and I developed renewed hope in our hearts for a privately rented flat. Also, the likelihood of Vicky's council flat beckoned something in the way of stability for our future.

We had burned a lot of floor-boards in the hovel-house, even forcing them up from the floor and breaking them to make a fire when we were desperate for warmth. So now the place was more treacherous than ever. Approximately every fourth floor board was broken or missing. We tried to keep ourselves well-groomed and clean but the circumstances were difficult and we must have looked like filthy vagrants from the general every-day life of living as we did.

I was feral but I couldn't let the people at work know that. So, if my shift allowed it and the public house was already open, I would pass by there and wash myself. On the shifts when I needed to be at work early, before the pub opened, I would have to go into work as I was. Thankfully there was a staff area down in the basement and away from the main source of hustle and bustle. If I was lucky, I could get in and down to the staff toilets, before being noticed by anyone. I would use the toilet and then quickly wash my face and pick the black from under my nails. Then I would take my tooth brush and paste from my jacket pocket and give my teeth a good clean.

This system worked well and I was only rarely caught in the act. If I behaved like I was doing nothing unusual then I could get away with it and as far as I knew I was not discussed for my unorthodox etiquette. No one knew that I was homeless except for Paul who'd gotten me the job in the first place. He had himself been in a similar position to me until his girlfriend had given birth. Now they'd been housed in a council flat and his old home had been flattened. We kept quiet about what we knew about each other and what had happened between us was never spoken of again.

Except for the hard work, random shifts and always stinking of burger-fat, in some ways I enjoyed working at McDonald's. There were a variety of different types working there. Some were full-time employees like me who'd ended up there for a variety of reasons. These were all Londoners, born and bred, except for me. Some were out of area part-time students who were only working there to boost their student grants up. We were all from different walks of life but the one thing we had in common was that we were all in our youth.

I received a uniform and an allowance every-day for food i.e., free burgers. There was a washing machine that I could use to wash my uniforms. I had the company of new acquaintances and it was warm. I could use the toilet whenever I needed and the wash room sinks were there for my use. At the end of two weeks I received my wages, eighty pounds which meant I was earning forty pounds per week. I tried to save as much as I could to go towards a deposit for a flat and rent that we would need in advance.

As I was still in my teens and therefore still in my formative years, my accent changed rapidly and as I spent a lot of time with Vicky and my McDonald's colleagues, I inevitably picked up a London twang. During this time I made a deliberate effort to rid myself of my Worcester accent. To shake off the sound of my voice that told the world where I came from. I wanted to strike Worcester's treacherous maze off the map, to pretend it never existed, that I'd never been there. If my accent sounded local I was less likely to be questioned about my reasons for being in London, stuff I wanted to forget.

Within a few months I'd probably lost fifty per cent of my Worcester accent. People started to assume I was from the local area on first meeting me but the true Londoners would soon pick up on an occasional word once I'd started to relax. After a few sentences they would sometimes ask me where I was from. But I would try to keep my answer brief and as vague as possible to prevent an onslaught of questions as to why I'd left Worcester.

With my wage and Vicky's allowance, we hoped we might be able to rent a flat. We commenced our search. With next to no deposit it was not going to be easy. I checked the shop window adverts every day in case any cheap flats came up for rent. Then one day in early July, I spotted one.

A one bedroom furnished flat. Only two weeks deposit and a month's rent in advance was demanded. If we could get on the right side of the landlord, it was within the realms of possibility that we might be able to secure it. I immediately went to the nearest pay phone and with my politest telephone voice I called the landlord. I discovered that the flat was above a model airplane shop, close to Crystal Palace train station and Sports centre.

We knew that we needed to act quickly and correctly or someone else would rent the flat before us. So, I arranged an immediate viewing that evening as I finished work. I had proof on me that I was in full time employment. Vicky had paperwork that proved she was in college, although she was on the point of leaving. We insisted the flat was acceptable to us (as beggars can't be choosers) and we convinced the landlord that we would be perfectly good tenants. With a lot of smiles in the right place, we managed to bypass the fact that we had no references from previous accommodation and a contract was drawn up for six months and signed with immediate effect.

We went straight back to the squat and said our thank yous and goodbyes to Bobby and Pete. We'd spent a good three months living, in absolute squalor, underneath two of the kindest men who ever lived. They had their own problems in this harsh world and had nothing much to give. But they'd kept an eye on us and kept us under their wings. We packed up our bags and left them as they stood at the squat door together, waving us off. I'll never forget the picture of them standing in front of that derelict building. With the boarded-up windows behind them. It's a tragic scene. Vicky and I had no way of keeping in touch with Bobby and Pete, other than going back to the squats. They'd be forced to leave there soon. We hoped we'd see them again but of course we never did.

Our new place was really a one bedroomed flat with a living room but the living room had a bed with cushions against the wall for use as a makeshift settee. So we decided to have no living room and instead we would have the luxury of having a bedroom each. There was a decent sized kitchen with a table and chairs and a shower room with a toilet. The place was fully furnished albeit with rotten old furniture but we were not complaining. This was the best place we'd lived in for a while and we were thrilled with it and pleased with ourselves for securing it.

The day after moving was my day off. We had empty kitchen cupboards to fill so it was time to go food shopping. I went by myself to a small supermarket that was next door to McDonald's on the high street. On the way there I dropped off our washing in the launderette. Vicky had shown me how to use the machines on a few occasions when we'd been to a different one, while living in the squats. I put the clothes in the machine and bough a small packet of washing powder from a dispenser. Then I loaded the washing and added the washing powder in one slot and the coins in another. While the machine was doing its job, I made my way to the small supermarket.

This was really my first proper trip to a supermarket where I had been responsible for choosing a proper weekly shop. At the squats, as there was no fridge or food-store facilities, we had mainly lived on chips, pre-packaged sandwiches and cakes. But now we had cupboards and a fridge and a cooker. I had been to the supermarkets many times with my mum, of course, but I'd not taken much notice of what she'd placed in the shopping trolley.

I picked up a shopping basket and started to place items into it. A bottle of coke, we would need something to drink. Some crisps and some chocolate. This didn't look right. Bread yes definitely bread was important and what else. What about some fruit or vegetables. I grabbed a bag of apples. As I waited in the queue to be served, I noticed sweets and chocolates strategically placed to grab the attention of children, to the despair of their parents. I took a packet of sweets and added it to the shopping basket. I was literally a child in a sweet shop. It's not that I didn't know which foods were good and bad, I just had little inclination to take care of myself.

After paying for the shopping, I returned to the launderette and finished off drying the clothes in a huge tumble-dryer. With one large bag of clean laundry on one arm and a bag of shopping in the other, I returned to our new flat.

Vicky had been out to meet up with her social worker but she was back now. She sat in the kitchen while I unpacked the bag from the supermarket. She seemed happy enough with the shopping items and we made ourselves a crisp-sandwich without any butter as I hadn't thought of buying that. We washed it down with a cup of coke.

'I hates social workers, don't you?' Oops, I'd reverted into my Worcester accent again!

'Ha, you sound like a farmer again, you're so funny!' Vicky laughed. 'Nah actually my social worker's pretty good, you know, on the ball, shit-hot'

Vicky was itching to tell me her news. Firstly, she'd just found out that she'd come first in her typing class, which was amazing seeing as she'd started at the bottom. And then about the meeting.

And so, she began. 'So, I've met up wiv me social-worker today and (she paused for effect) I'm getting a council flat! - Well I've not got it yet but I'm definitely getting it in October!'

'That's the best news ever!!!' I squealed, 'Wow, things are really looking up for us'

'Yeah so, I need to start preparing all the stuff I'll be needing, the social's gonna help me with getting furniture and stuff' Vicky looked me straight in the eye, she was telling me something without saying it.

'Oh, erm, where is it?' My thoughts were racing as I realised Vicky was no longer referring to the council-flat as 'our place.' She'd started to refer to it as her council-flat now and I realised that when she was allocated a place, she would not be taking me with her. She had a new boyfriend and he was taking priority over me of late. I assumed she was rejecting me, something I was used to by now but I was thrown into a quandary.

'Kennington' She simply replied. And that was the end of the conversation. Now I knew that I was on my own.

Vicky was indeed planning to leave me, I needed to think about what I would do next. Even if I could find someone else to share this flat with me, our landlord was not going to renew the contract at the end of the six months. So I would need to find somewhere else to go then anyway. At least I had some time to try and work something out.

One of the students that worked part-time in the burger bar had taken an interest in me. His name was Marty, three years my senior and a student on a degree course at a local prestigious art college. Marty seemed to be a lovely, kind guy. He was small in stature, but he owned a big heart. He was living just around the corner from Vicky and I, in a huge, Edwardian, rented house with eight other art students. He was obviously attracted to me but although I really enjoyed his company, unfortunately, I was physically unattracted to him.

Marty obviously fancied me but it seemed more than just that. He seemed to really care. On many occasions he suggested that I should go back to school and retake my leaver's exams. He said I was intelligent enough to do it. I thought about his comments. I used to be clever but that was a long time ago and I'd since missed out on a lot of education. And anyway, how would I support myself? If I worked full-time with shifts then I would have no time to study and attend college. If I worked part time then I could not afford to support myself. Full-time degree students, like Marty, could afford to work part-time as they were in receipt of a substantial student grant and of course they had parents to fall back on if need be.

I looked into my options on the possibility of going to college. There were no fees to pay to complete the school-leaver's certificates (Ordinary levels) for those under the age of nineteen. This level of education should normally be completed at school and by the age of sixteen. After the age of nineteen I'd have to pay to take these certificates and that would be costly. So, if I were to ever get these leavers qualifications, there was no time like the present. But I wasn't entitled to any kind of living grant for this lower level of education as it was assumed that students would still live at their parents' address.

The only way for me to manage it would be to stop working altogether and claim out-of-work benefits again. I'd recently learned that I could claim for rent on top of money to live on. The benefits office rule was that the college lessons must not exceed twenty-two hours per week. And I was still to seek fulltime employment, overwise my money could be stopped. This wasn't an ideal way to enter education but I went ahead and enrolled for O-level certificates at Southwark College in central London. The course would commence in September.

Every day when Marty came into work, he would come directly over to me with a big smile on his face. He knew that my eighteenth birthday was fast approaching and was saddened to hear that I had nothing planned for the milestone day.

'I've been thinking about your birthday', Marty started, 'You got anything planned yet?'

I shook my head. 'No' I replied simply.

'Well, I've been telling the other students, in my house, about you and,' he hesitated, 'and, well what about we have a party at ours - for you?'

'Oh wow, yes, that would be nice but the problem is I don't know anyone, I mean, I wouldn't know any of the people at my own party, would I?' I felt a mixture of elation and confusion.

'Well I wanted to invite you to meet my friends anyway, whenever you have time.' He added.

I was intrigued and touched by Marty's idea.

CHAPTER 6

Sunny

It was the end of August and I'd been invited to Marty's digs. He'd given me a piece of paper with the address scribbled on it. Number 11, Cintra Park. I knew roughly where to find the street. I was looking out for a large, Edwardian, semi-detached house. Marty had already told me that it had five stories and nine bedrooms!

I was pretty punctual and as I was about to knock, the door opened and Marty was there, grinning from ear to ear. Most of his house-mates were hanging out in one of the larger rooms on the second floor. Marty eagerly led me in and then up two flights of stairs.

Most of the occupants were male with only a couple of female students. They were a funny, crazy lot of young people, full of enthusiasm for life and London and all things arty and interesting. Most of them were about to go into their second year at the art college. None of them were Londoners originally, only migrating there to study their passion, graphic design, fashion and fine art.

Showing interest in Marty's new friend, the art-students gathered around me. Several of them were very well spoken with, what I guessed were, home-counties accents. A couple of the guys commenced polite conversation with me. One called Jimmy was particularly entertaining. He was so kind and polite. He cracked jokes to make me feel at ease. I was just starting to settle as one of the female students interrupted.

'Which course are you on?' The girl enquired. I guessed she was one of the fashion students, by her huge, brightly coloured material bow she wore around her head and the unusual eye makeup.

'Oh, I don't go to your college.' I replied as I looked at Marty for assistance.

'No, Jenny's a friend of mine from Macdonald's.' Marty said.

'Oh, so you work part time with Marty at the burger bar, oh I see, so which college do you go to then?' She continued.

'Erm, no I, I work full time at Macdonald's but I am planning on going to college in September' I replied. I hoped my semi confident answer would end this topic of conversation. Something about this girl's tone made me feel awkward.

'What are you going to study in September then?' the fashion girl continued. She had a confused look on her face as she struggled to pigeonhole me.

'Erm, I'm going to do O'levels?' I don't know why I made it sound like a question.

'You mean school leaving certificates? How old are you?' Both of these questions were obviously rhetorical so I just shrugged my shoulders without answering. She seemed genuinely perplexed as she continued 'Why? Why didn't you take the school leaving certificates at - for example - school?' She smirked and looked at the others for their reactions. With a bemused expression she continued, 'Why would you want to work full time in a burger bar?' She went cross eyed and shook her head.

I felt myself shuffling on my seat. In this predominantly male environment she was obviously the Queen Bee. Unbeknown to me she was threatened by my mere presence. She was doing a good job of making me feel unwelcome while Marty did his best to counteract her dialogue.

'Do you want a beer, Jen?' Marty interrupted.

'Maybe Jenny would like a cup of tea?' A pleasant ginger haired young man named Aaron, added.

With that the Queen Bee turned and started making conversation with the other female. I was relieved and continued to enjoy the company of the worker bees.

Although I enjoyed the art students' company, I felt I was beneath them. They all had proven intelligence with a string of Ordinary levels certificates each and Advanced levels plus a gift for the arts. It was no mean feat to be offered a place at that particular college of art and design and one or two of them were full of themselves with an air of arrogance for their amazing achievement in this world. They'd done well, that was true, but most of them had no understanding of my kind of history. And why would they understand it, it made no sense - even to me.

Marty tried to understand. He was very kind and caring. He was keen to help me to find somewhere else to live as it was apparent that Vicky would be going off without me, shortly. He hoped that I could rent a room in the student house. The problem was that many of the other students, from the art college, wanted a room there too. If a room became available, there was always a queue of others ready and willing and keen to take it. Obviously, art students from the same college would have priority over me, in the eyes of everyone else except Marty.

The student house had five floors from the attic to the basement. Every floor had two double bedrooms except for the basement. The basement had only one double room and a tiny room that would have been the original old coal room, when the

Edwardian building was first built. Now the house had central heating and coal was no longer used, so it was left as an empty cupboard. It was a tiny room with a little hatch where the coal would have been thrown into the building in the old days. The coal would've been pulled through the hatch and sorted out in this room. The students referred to this room as 'the coal hole' as it was nothing more than that.

Vicky was making plans to leave our place and I was keen to find somewhere else to stay. There were two Irish girls, renting a ground floor flat in the same street as the student house. One of them was planning on going back to Ireland and the other was urgently looking for a flat-mate. Marty knew them and introduced me and I moved in within days.

It was a small ground floor flat, located at the other end of the street called Cintra Park. Luckily it had a telephone, so I gave the number to Vicky. We would make every effort to keep in touch and to meet up from time to time. I was to share a room in the one bedroomed flat, with an Irish girl called Catherine, two years my senior. She was an intelligent, articulate girl, tall, slim with long mousy-blonde hair. She'd come to London with her friend to make her fortune as a photographer. Her friend had already given up and gone back home to Dublin but Catherine was still trying to make it.

Catherine came from a totally different background to me. She'd been born and raised a catholic in Dublin. She told me her family had been 'piss-poor' but had the 'love of God' and 'each other' to keep them sustained. She was always on the phone to loads of brothers and sisters back in Ireland. We had nothing much in common but we got along well.

The same week as I moved in with Catherine, I stopped working at MacDonalds and started attending lessons at college. Now every day I would take the train from Crystal Palace into London Bridge train station, to attend my lessons at Southwark collage of further education.

Every morning as I passed through the station I'd say 'Good Morning!' to the friendly train-guard. And then one day my train was delayed and we got chatting. He was probably fifteen years older than me, dark skinned with a big, smile. At first, I struggled to understand his Caribbean accent. He seemed to miss out a lot of connecting words and he spoke very fast. It took a while to tune into. But eventually I understood that he originated from Trinidad and that his friends called him Sunny. It was obvious why they called him Sunny, he was like the Sunshine! Always super smiley and friendly. I don't think I've met a happier train-guard before or since. He really made an impression on me. A little happy mark on my broken heart.

'Sunny - yesterday my life was filled with rain'

Sunny -you smiled at me and really eased the pain'

'Oh, the dark days are gone and the bright days are here'

'My Sunny one shines so sincere'

'Sunny one so true, I love you'

I always had that song in my head after seeing Sunny. I skipped through the station like I'd taken a pick-me-up. He was a sight for sore eyes. A real tonic.

I was now studying for the certificates that I should've gotten from school. I enjoyed my days at college and most evenings Catherine and I would socialize with the art students. I knew that Marty liked me a lot and although I cared about him as a friend, there was no physical attraction on my part.

However, I was interested in another one of the students - Jimmy. He was a tall dark and handsome young man who'd come to London to study Graphic Design and have the time of his life! He came from a privileged background of private schooling and middle-class aspirations. He'd shown interest and kindness towards me on the occasions when I'd come into contact with him.

The day before my eighteenth birthday, I went to collage as usual. And as always, I got chatting with Sunny, while I waited on the platform. Of course, I managed to slip it into the conversation that tomorrow would be my birthday! And he smiled and joked with me in his typical jovial manner. He really was an asset to the train company. He brought sunshine and joy to many a grey morning in south east London. It was like he'd brought the Trinidadian weather with him. Not that I'd ever witnessed Trinidadian weather. In fact, before I'd met Sunny, I'd never even heard of Trinidad. I didn't even know where it was on the world map.

My birthday came on a Wednesday at the end of September. As I passed through the train station, Sunny was standing in his little ticket both, smiling from ear to ear. 'Appy Birday, little someting ere yuh goin grocery, nah dou worry dou worry' And with that indecipherable statement, he thrust a small box of chocolates into my hands. Well, this was just so kind and so thoughtful! I was absolutely shocked and thrilled.

I would never forget Sunny.

I received some interesting handmade cards, one from Marty and another two from a couple of the other students. I knew Marty had cajoled them into this effort but I appreciated it all the same. They were so talented.

CHAPTER 7

Coming Of Age

Then the Saturday evening came and it was time for my party! Initially, I met up with Marty, and a few of the graphic design students, in a local pub. But within half an hour the place was overflowing with trendy fashion students and those on other art courses from the college. They all obviously knew one another as they screamed their in-jokes with excitement on meeting. Every now and then, Marty would shout over and interrupt their greetings and insist they learn my name.

'This is Jenny,' he'd shout over the background music and the chatter. 'It's Jenny's eighteenth!'

Most of the students were polite and friendly although I detected some nonchalance and some confusion as to my unknown face. I soon started to feel overwhelmed by the situation. I was being introduced to so many new faces on the celebration of this important birthday. I didn't know this environment; I didn't know the people around me and I didn't know the rules of engagement. I suddenly felt bombarded with tangled up emotions that I couldn't explain.

With hindsight, I guess it was bereavement at the loss of my mother, every other family member, my pets, every friend and every place I'd ever known. This coupled with an element of awkwardness and embarrassment.

I started to feel an unexplained lump in my throat so I took a swing of my Bacardi and Coke.

Marty noticed something was up. 'You, ok?'

Then his sympathy caused my confused tears to flow and my embarrassment doubled. What must everyone think of this unknown character now! I surmised.

Marty put his arm around me. 'What's wrong? It's your eighteenth! You're meant to be happy!' he continued as others tried not to stare. They politely turned their backs and chatted in amongst themselves.

'I don't know' I replied. And I honestly didn't know.

Another one of the guys went straight to the bar and got another round of drinks in. He suggested that I knock mine back quickly and then we'd all make our way back to the house. I downed another Bacardi and started to feel calmer.

Number 11 filled up quickly with over a hundred

art students from the college. With my anxiety suppressed, I spoke to lots of them. The majority had no idea that this was meant to be someone's birthday party! Apparently, parties at the house were a regular occurrence. When I told different groups that it was my eighteenth, they generally insisted that I take a can of lager from their pack or a plastic cup full of cheap wine. I started to relax more and soon I began to really enjoy myself. I'd found myself in amongst friendly, intelligent and incredibly interesting young people.

With the confidence of alcohol in my veins, I socialised, danced and sang out loud with the others. As well as an abundance of booze, there was freely available cannabis and other stuff. I had a dabble and totally lost myself in the moment. I felt free as a bird that evening. Or perhaps more like high as a kite. For a while I actually believed that I was an art student too, having the time of my life.

I remember the excitement of flirting with Jimmy but after that I was completely plastered and he was too, by all accounts. So, I had minimal recollection of that first night of passion. But usually, for those moments, I would have felt so special, so important, so loved, euphoric. I would have been convinced I filled up all of his senses and I must have thrown caution to the wind. But that euphoria overwhelmed reason in my adolescent brain. That euphoria was just nature's cruel joke. Nature's enticement to lure me to repeatedly dice with danger. Love (if you can call it that) is a drug.

Jimmy must have embraced me all night as I do remember waking up in his strong arms. He was Mister Romance himself, full of politeness and obligatory good morning/goodbye kisses. Jimmy would've been happy enough with a one-night stand and in that scenario the other person has no say.

Our drunken night together upset Marty of course. I felt guilty and sorry for that. But I wanted a relationship with Jimmy. I was to be disappointed.

Jimmy used to refer to me as 'the girl next door' partially because I was technically his neighbour. And I suppose he meant that I was 'nothing special,' an ordinary girl, not special enough for him. Anyway, he wasn't looking for a relationship and even if he was, it wasn't going to be with me. But I didn't understand males. I stupidly thought that if they 'made love' to you that meant they loved you and everything else would just fall into place. No one had taught me that when you give 'your all' too soon, you risk every type of rejection and misery. I was already an addict - addicted to the rush of new beginnings. A hopeless case.

I was just eighteen and now officially an adult. I was already broken and damaged in so many ways but my experience with Jimmy threw me into a new state of chaos and dilemma, which I was ill equipped to deal with. I wanted a relationship, to belong to someone and to stop being alone in this cold world. His kind demeanour and posh accent disguised the obvious, that I was just a series of notches on the bedpost to him. But was there more? Catherine said this seed of hope must be destroyed. 'Don't ya go breaking ya 'art over that one, he's just out for the crack so he his' I really didn't know what she was saying half the time!

Jimmy's friends advised me that I was far too young to be settled down. That there was plenty of time for all that in the future. That now was the time for enjoying my youth! That Jimmy was not the settling down type and that he was too young at only twenty-one. That it was all my fault for getting myself into this mess in the first place. That getting out of it wouldn't be so traumatic.

As the months passed, Catherine increasingly missed her family and became despondent due to her lack of success in the harsh photography world in London. She soon followed her friend in also deciding to go back to live with her parents in Dublin. She left in the middle of December to make sure she was back with her big Irish family for a good old-fashioned Christmas. Which meant that I was about to be alone for Christmas.

Jimmy must have felt some responsibility towards me and offered for me to go with him to his parent's home in the Home Counties. I guess he'd told them that I was a 'just a friend,' this 'orphan girl' who he felt sorry for. And they were kind enough to agree to my stay.

It's awkward staying with other people's families, especially at Christmas. Although I felt physically sick and mentally unwell, I did my best to act happy and I hid my dilemma. I was never really sure of Jimmy's true feelings towards me. But he'd made it clear he wanted nothing serious, nothing exclusive. Not with me anyway.

'By the look in your eye, I can tell you're gonna cry,'

'Is it over me? If it is, save your tears cause I'm not worth it you see'

That's a song that would always remind me of Jimmy but I bet when he heard it, he never gave me a second thought.

Jimmy was devilishly handsome and I was not the only girl who thought so. Several threw themselves at him. But he was far from being the devil himself. Moreover, he was just too polite to refuse female advances even if he wasn't overly attracted. He wouldn't want to offend. He was cursed with middle class politeness and an extremely courteous demeanour. A gentle and kind approach towards females which I'd mistaken for something else. He was always centre stage for me - while the real devil waited in the wings.

Jimmy couldn't help himself and I didn't even blame him. He was a victim of his own good looks and male hormones. I was a victim of my sex drive too but of course; I had a bigger price to pay. I can't even say that we ever broke up as we were never a real couple in the first place. I suppose you could say that we remained friends of a kind. He was happy go lucky and clearly had no hesitation and no regrets.

In the January I drew a line under it all. Hope was gone. Now it was time to move forwards. Onwards and upwards as they say.

Marty had been pretty upset with Jimmy and I. He'd invested a lot of time and effort in me. His feelings had gotten involved and he'd been hurt. He'd done all the groundwork and been pipped to the post for the prise, by his housemate. He must have felt a fool. He'd introduced Jimmy to me in the first place and I'd been hurt and damaged by the whole episode. Poor Marty had been privy to it all. But Marty was a dear and his sympathy trumped his sadness. He was loving and giving and he soon forgave the both of us.

After that horrible episode with Jimmy was over, I started to spiral downwards mentally but I guess no one could see it. In reality, I was standing on the edge of adulthood but I was still a child - in a woman's body. I certainly was not ready for adult independence. Since my mother had died, when I was fifteen, all of my energy had gone into grieving and the effort of repeatedly moving house. All the while an abundance of female hormones was building up and driving my desire for physical affection and a need to be loved. This combined chaos had caused my maturity to stall like I hadn't completed emotional finishing school or something. In some ways I never did grow up. I was eternally stuck at fifteen.

Now and then (too often) I would develop an obsession for a certain guy, causing me to feel an abnormal zest for life and an almost uncontrolled excitement. An affliction materialised that attached itself as a manic infatuation. I would throw myself into a relationship without caution and give myself away in virtually no time at all. In return I was generally accepted and rejected, leaving me with a crushing depression that led to a suicidal awakening. As I recovered, I would repeat the cycle of extreme manic happiness followed by appalling despair and misery and a crushing depression and then several days or even weeks of self-inflicted starvation. I would just be so destressed that I couldn't chew. My appetite would disappear and then I'd be unable to eat to the point of having to force myself. My weight would drop drastically during these episodes.

By the May, my exams were in full swing. I came back to the flat one day and noticed, from outside, that all of the lights were on. I was confused. Had I left the lights on? Had Catherine come back? Had the landlord arrived to relet the place? I entered with trepidation and immediately felt the answer. The place was a mess, I'd been burgled. My stuff was spread across the floor and there was a feeling of someone else's presence.

Afraid, I ran down the street to the student house and explained what had happened. Two of the male students, kindly came back with me to check out the flat. I didn't have much but what was worth anything was missing. Twenty pounds cash was gone and a radio which I'd bought for myself. I was a vulnerable young woman living alone in a ground floor flat with a dodgy back window and the flat entrance hidden from view. It was a failsafe mission for the burglars, like taking candy from a baby.

CHAPTER 8

Coal-Hole

I didn't want to stay at the flat now and felt scared and was crying like a child. The two male students took me with them to their house for the time being while they tried to think of what to do with me. All the rooms in the student house were occupied except for the uninhabitable one - the coal-hole. There was a house meeting and it was agreed that the coal-hole could be made into a tiny bedroom for me. The only one left to clear it with was Mister Patel, the Asian landlord. I was to get my things and move in first and we would clear it with the landlord after the event. Desperate times called for desperate measures.

I didn't have a bed so the same two male students took the single one for me from the burgled flat. Marty and some other art students helped with the carrying of the rest of my stuff. A worn-out orange suit case and several carrier bags did the trick.

The coal-hole had a normal sized door, so the guys managed to get the bed in without too much trouble. It took up two thirds of the room, leaving little space to maneuverer. I pushed the majority of my belongings under the bed and there was space for a bag at the end, in front of the coal-hatch. There was an electric light-bulb hanging down and a tiny window, not big enough to get your head through. Looking through that tiny basement window all that could be seen was a brick wall about a metre away. I nudged one of my plastic clothes bags over as I opened the low-down tiny hatch. Inside was a black slanted wall covered in the black residue of the old coal. I closed the door quickly, I didn't like it one bit, it scared me. I left a clothes bag in front of the hatch to block it and prevent it from spontaneously opening.

When Mister Patel came to collect his weekly rent money, he found out that I'd moved into the coal-hole. I was amazed as he agreed that I could stay. I was to pay him £10 per week. This was half of what the others were paying for the double rooms. Marty assured me that one of the double rooms would be coming available soon and I would be next in line to get it. The coal-hole was very claustrophobic so I hoped it would be sooner rather than later. I found it difficult to sleep in there and started to have horrendous nightmares.

I managed to attend all of my exams at college but the burglary and house move had hindered my studying and inevitably, my scores. However, I did manage some revision and passed all of my exams with very average C's. I knew I would have done better if I hadn't gone through that 'relationship' with Jimmy. But that was in the past now. So, I re-enrolled for three Advanced levels (A levels) and vowed to improve next time.

Marty was a great artist and an amazing guitarist. I would often go to his room, in the attic of the house, where he would play and we would sing harmonies together. He said that I had a good singing voice and a pitch-perfect musical ear. It reminded me of when I used to sing with my family, in the car, on our trips out together. I thought about my old house in my old street called Holly-mount and the treacherous maze of Worcester. I wondered if anyone was thinking of me there or if I'd been reported missing? - I had not.

The double room, in the basement next to my tiny room, became available. Marty was keen for me to get it as he understood how horrible and impractical it was in the coal-hole. A pretty, first year female student called Jaz was also fighting my corner. But there were others that were insisting that another first year student had been waiting for a while and she should take priority over me. This caused a rift in the house. Trouble broke out between a male student and Jaz. Jaz got so angry in the heated row, that she actually cried out of pity for me. But eventually she was forced to back down and the new girl moved in to the empty room next to mine. Jaz really had tried hard to secure me the room and I admired her for it. We started to chat a lot and she'd often invite me up to her double room on the second floor. We started to become good friends.

My nineteenth birthday passed with drinks in a Crystal Palace pub and my confused emotions. Jaz was perplexed and again, I could not explain what I felt 'Oh, she always cries on her birthday' I overheard a female voice say. I wasn't sure who but I suspected the Queen bee.

Apart from being in the coal-hole, there was generally a nice atmosphere in the student house and I started to feel a kind of belonging. It was a house full of life and excitement. These young people, of which I was the youngest, were having the time of their lives. From down in the basement, I'd often hear some commotion followed by screeches of laughter. I'd smile to myself and then go and investigate. Then I'd usually end up passing my time chatting and joking in one of the other rooms. Or a group of us might decide to go off to a local pub. On warmer days we'd sometimes go to the local Crystal Palace Park with a few beers. It was all very pleasant and diverting.

For half terms and end of term breaks, the students would all go home to stay with their respective families. As Christmas approached, I realised that I would be spending it alone in the huge

Edwardian house and so I tried to prepare myself mentally. As all of the other students were getting ready to go home, Jaz kindly offered for me to stay in her double room during the time she'd be away, instead of the coal-hole. I gladly took her up on this offer. At the age of nineteen, it would be my very first Christmas alone, although I'd felt alone at all of the different addresses since my mother's death.

By Christmas eve all of the students had gone and the huge Edwardian house fell silent and eerie. I went out to the minimarket and got a few things in to eat. A couple of cans of lager, a packet of crisps, a box of mince pies and a small Christmas pudding for one.

I spent the evening drinking lager and watching all of the usual Christmas programs on Jaz's television. Christmas morning, I woke up and made myself a cup of tea with slightly off-milk which someone had left in the fridge. I cracked open a mince pie and watched more television. The scenes of perfect happy families, roasting chestnuts on an open fire and memories of my childhood Christmases, were all a bit too much for me. It was a rotten time and I vowed never to spend Christmas alone again.

When Jaz came back after New Year's Day, I begrudgingly made my way back to my coal-hole. After a few minutes there was a knock on my door. Jaz came in and sat on my bed with me. She'd been having a think about me over Christmas. She'd de-

88

cided that if I wanted, I could bring my bed up to her double room and we would share and split the Twenty-pound rent. This was amazing news and I enthusiastically accepted without hesitation.

Then the two of us somehow managed to lift my single bed up two flights of stairs from the basement to the first floor. It took us far longer than it should have as we laughed and joked and struggled with its weight. I felt so happy and relieved to be out of the coal-hole.

I would share the double room with Jaz. Our two single beds on opposite walls, in the double room, on the second floor of the huge old house. We intended to split the twenty-pound rent so it would cost me the same amount as I'd paid in the coal-hole, that being £10.

However, because we honestly and stupidly told the landlord we were sharing, he insisted we pay £30 for the room which meant £15 each. I felt bad for Jaz as she'd kindly offered to give up half of her room, out of sympathy for me, but ended up losing her privacy and space while still having to pay almost the same rent. I was so glad to be out of the coal-hole though and Jaz appreciated how grateful I was and seemed content with her decision. She was a very positive person in her outlook in life in general. A private-school girl from a steady and happy family. Her positivity rubbed off on me.

Jaz and I became great friends. We would sit up

and chat in our room. Sometimes we would watch Jaz's television or play with the record player her parents had given to her. We would chat for hours and make plans to travel together one day. She came from Bristol and she sometimes invited me to go with her to stay at her parents' house and on occasion, I went. Her parents were lovely, happily married and financially stable as well as content. I felt welcome and almost part of the family; they were quite relaxed and easy-going. They seemed happy for me to visit and stay whenever Jaz went home although obviously not by myself.

CHAPTER 9

Whirlwind

Jaz was on the committee of the student union and she made a fake student identification card for me. With this I could attend all of the student gigs at the college for free or next to nothing. I'd happily pretend to be one of the art students and like that I enjoyed a great social life with my housemates. I almost fitted in, although I never really was one of them. I wouldn't have described myself as a hanger-oner as people seemed to enjoy my company, I was more like the blended family pet.

Jaz had a male friend, a fellow Graphic Design student in her year, whose name was Rob. Unusually, for the students, he still lived at home with his parents in a nearby area. He came from a steady and secure family, which was probably exactly the kind of guy I needed. He was an A grade student, a year or two older than myself and an all-round thoroughly decent bloke. I'd met him at a couple of student gigs and he started to visit us at the house. As Rob was tall, clever, extremely talented and funny, I found him attractive and we took an interest in one other. Then a whirlwind romanced commenced. This innocent one, fell head-over-heels in love with me. And for a while I thought I loved him too.

In the beginning everything was romantic and we had a lot of fun together going to student parties and pubs. But as the relationship went from fun to something deeper, I felt myself disconnecting and I never really knew why. I guess I just couldn't relate to that amount of normalness. Moreover, I felt Rob couldn't understand me, my temperament, my ups and downs. It was like we came from different planets. When I got upset about things such as the death of my mother or my complicated memories of my estranged father and sister, he'd just tell me to 'get over it' or to 'be happy.' His uneventful life had understandably caused him to have zero comprehension of anything that I'd been through.

Although older than me, Rob was young and inexperienced by comparison. His lack of life knowledge and compassion became abundantly clearer as the months went on and I started to withdraw from him. The more I withdrew, the more he attached himself to me.

It was Easter and I guess Rob could feel what was coming. I hadn't been right with him in recent weeks. Someone else had let him in through the main door of the house and then there was a knock on my bedroom door. I instinctively knew it was him. I'd made my decision. I couldn't go on stringing him along and I needed to tell him it was over. As I opened the bedroom door, what was about to happen must have been written on my face.

Rob was standing there holding a little, woven wicker-basket. Over the preceding days he'd made it himself. Then he'd gone to all the shops in his area to find different chocolate eggs. The basket was filled with a variety of mini chocolate eggs and ribbons. It was spectacular, artistic and thoughtful. But as I opened the door, and before I'd even noticed the basket, my face said 'it's over.' Rob immediately got nervous and the basket slipped from his grasp. It hit the floor and broke and all of the little eggs started rolling. Next, we were both on our hands and knees on the floor picking the eggs up. It was awful as I still had to tell him we were through. He came into my room and we sat on my bed and I said what I had to say.

Rob was clearly devastated. His life was no longer 'uneventful' because of me and I was riddled with guilt. After he left, I sat on my bed holding the eggs in the broken basket. I sat there worrying about him and deciding if I'd done the right thing. But really, I had no choice.

It's just so ironic that damaged people can only connect with the damaged in romantic relationships. This is the reason that those cultures who deal in arranged marriages, avoid picking spouses for their grown-up children from broken homes. It seems hash to write someone off because of their parent's divorce or other previous difficulties in life. But it makes sense to me now.

I probably encountered loads of decent guys like Rob, who would've tried to love me and to give me a good life but I guess I didn't speak their language and eventually they would realise that they didn't speak mine.

I could have decent male friends; I could have relationships with good guys too. But it looked like it would only last up until the end of the honeymoon period. As it progressed from 'in love' to deeper love, the language changed and so did the culture and then a disconnect. Well, that's what happened with Rob anyway. I'm sorry to Rob. I know he never, ever forgave me for hurting him like that. But I would get what was coming. I would get my comeuppance.

Over the following couple of weeks, I received two heart-breaking letters from Rob. They were both extremely well written. His level of education was obviously far superior to mine. His articulate and heart-felt emotion flowed from his pen almost like the genius of Shakespeare. It was really hard to read and I had to keep taking breaks to be able to cope with the pain I'd caused him. Bizarrely, on the back of the final page, he'd drawn a picture of his manhood. It was incredibly detailed and accurate. But why he'd done this, I couldn't comprehend. Perhaps he wanted to draw my attention to what I was missing? I guess he just wasn't in his right mind at the time. But it kind of summed up our relationship. Rob was loving, kind, intelligent, well-educated and extremely talented. But there was the immaturity and the disconnect. From there the relationship ceased.

One of the students, in the house, was a lovely, funny and arty guy called Aaron. Tall and slim with ginger hair and good looking, albeit in a quirky way. Soon after my whirlwind romance was over, we began to become good friends. It was a warm spring and we went through a phase of taking an old, checked blanket out to the overgrown garden of the house. We would flatten the long grass down with it. Then we'd take it in turns to go into the back kitchen of the house and make cups of tea to bring outside. We spent many hours talking rubbish and drinking tea. We made each other laugh. I felt a connection to him, like brother and sister almost.

Aaron knew I'd loved the ballet and so one day he suggested we go to the Royal Opera House in Covent Garden to see a performance. We didn't have much money but at that time it was possible to pay £4 to stand up and watch from the back of the theatre.

As soon as I walked in, I felt like I'd come home. I

truly loved the ballet and the theatre. We saw the Royal ballet company perform Romeo and Juliet. Aaron was so tall; he could see easily but I had to stand on my tip-toes. But from what I could see, it was a magical and wonderful performance.

We were on a high after the show. We went and got something to eat from the cheapest pie takeaway stand we could find. It was a wonderful day and I realised that my love for the dance had not died although physically (and nearing the age of twenty) it was already too late for me to become a ballerina. I realised that all of my teenage dreams had been pie in the sky.

Many wild parties came and went in the Edwardian house. Once we all went on a bus to a toga party, at another student house, wearing old sheets. Another party involved us all dressing up as the opposite sex. This was easy enough for us girls, we would just rummage through the boys cupboards until we found a suitable shirt and maybe draw on a moustache or beard. There was more work involved for the boys. They would have to make trips to the charity shops to purchase suitably large dresses. Marty found himself a lovely pink mini dress and Aaron got a gold maxi dress with a slit up the side which showed off his hairy legs. Some thought it didn't show enough leg though so while we waited at the bus stop, Jimmy ripped it all the way up to the top. Aaron was left showing the whole length of his legs and underpants but he was so gentle and laid-back and wasn't bothered in the slightest.

On my happier days I often instigated wild behaviour back at the house. Marty would play his guitar and we would all sit around chatting and singing.

'11 Cintra park is the best'

'11 Cintra park is the greatest'

'The kitchen is always a mess,'

'And there's no toilet-roll in the toilet'

I don't know who'd made that song up. It didn't even rhyme! Still, that didn't stop us from singing it!

Then one of us would shout out 'tin trunk, tin trunk' and that meant it was time for us to take it in turns getting unto the trunk in Aaron's room. While one of us was in it, the others would bang on the top and the person inside would have to sing a song until they were let out.

I even managed to get on the good side of the Queen bee. I had a talent for finding the good in people. I believed that everyone had a story to tell. And it turned out that the Queen bee wasn't so bad after all. She was just full of determination to make it in the world of fashion and nothing would get in her way. I really admired her for that. Although I envied her because my dreams had been so cruelly trashed. She obviously wouldn't have understood that and just appeared to look down her nose at me. But I realised that everyone has good and bad in them. We all have our insecurities. We all have our history and stuff going on inside of us which we cannot explain. We're all slaves to our emotions which dictate our behaviours. I, for example, was stuck with guilt and sympathy for everyone. But it was what made me a people-person and I had no regrets about that.

Pubs, clubs, gigs, parties and some free movement in the bedrooms was rife. There were some secret liaisons and some not so secret. There were love-affairs and one-night stands. There were some great romances, great fun and some minor and major broken hearts. Some of us were so close we might sleep in bed together and nothing might happen. The boys were real gentlemen and would never push or insist even when a girl was next to them half naked. I spent several nights with Marty, just chatting and sleeping and the same with Aaron.

Unfortunately, every few months the landlord, Mr Patel, would threaten us with eviction. We were on a six monthly rolling contract and he would always threaten not to renew it. This had been the same procedure since the now 'third-years' had first moved in, in their first year at college. They were coming up to the end of their courses and the landlord was saying it was the end of the line for us all. This time the students seemed to be taking him seriously.

This is when a proper room (my own room) in the house finally became available and as the lease on the house was approaching the end, no one else was going for it. A male student moved out and I got his double room on the ground floor. It would have been a kind of luxury if only I could have concentrated on my studies instead of spending these last couple of months worrying where I'd be living next.

The deadline for our eviction would coincide with my A level exams. It was normal for three A level subjects to be studied with the final exams being after two years. But I was claiming out-of-work benefits to support myself and the dole office were on my back for me to get a job. So, as I was scared, they might stop my money at any time, I'd taken a one-year course instead of two years. A-levels were difficult, especially in such a compact course. I'd struggled to keep up, especially as the dole office kept calling me in for meetings and pressurising me to come off benefits. By the second term of the academic year, I'd already dropped two out of three of my subjects. Now I was left with only one subject.

Again, my overwhelming priority was finding somewhere to live. The other students did not concern themselves half as much. They all had a safety net of their parents to fall back on if the worst came to the worst. So, this rolling-stone way of life was more like an adventure to them than the hell it was to me. Every now and then they would check the newspapers and shop windows for any available properties to rent while I searched non-stop and worried incessantly at the expense of my college work.

By now the six third-year students had already graduated. They all intended to stay living in London with the aspiration of working in their chosen subjects of Graphic Design and Fashion. The six graduates decided to search for a smaller house to rent together, closer to central London. When they found somewhere, they left number 11, leaving three of us and only a month to go before termination of the contract and imminent eviction.

I'd already taken one section of the A level examination and was sure I'd not done well. Now all I could think about was housing and my obsession was preventing me from eating or attending lessons. The morning of the main part of the exam arrived and I just didn't bother to attend. I was angry and frustrated with myself but I had to find somewhere to live and that was all I could think of. Anyway, one A level would not have got me into university. Still having it would have been more of an achievement than not having it.

Disappointed with myself and realising that Jaz and the other second-year student would go off together without me, I went into central London one day looking for work and accommodation. Perhaps, if I were to be really lucky, I might find a job with accommodation.

I passed a public house called the Talbot, the nearest pub to Buckingham Palace. There was an urgent notice in the window asking for staff and the position was live-in. Perfect, just what I needed. I went in to inquire.

The Landlord of the Talbot was due to leave the establishment in a few days and to move on to a different public house. Apparently, he was taking his loyal staff with him but according to his publican's agreement, he was not meant to. He was supposed to leave a full team behind at the pub, ready to serve for the new landlord. If the landlord could leave at least one bar staff member behind, then he could get away with taking his other staff with him.

I'd never worked as a barmaid before but that didn't matter and the job was automatically mine. In the eleventh hour I'd landed on my feet with a job and accommodation all at the same time. So, I went back to the student house and called the dole office to inform them that I no longer needed their money as I was starting work. I said goodbye to the last couple of students and packed up my belongings.

I stood outside for a moment and looked up at the huge Edwardian house. I'd lived there for a year and that'd been my longest address in four years. I thought of all the parties and crazy times I'd had there. All the students I'd met there. It all seemed very quiet now. It was over.

Carrying my orange case and a couple of carrier bags, I walked a few steps in the direction of the train station. Then I stopped and looked back at the house again, for the last time. I guess 11 Cintra Park really was the best.

I hadn't been on the train for a couple of weeks so I hadn't seen Sunny. I hoped to see him to say good-bye on this day but as I passed through, he was nowhere to be seen and I guessed it was his day off. That was unfortunate.

CHAPTER 10

Twenty

I had a nice big room at the Talbot in Victoria, central London and I was living next door to the Queen! The public house was at the bottom of the rear gardens of the extensive grounds of Buckingham Palace. I was neighbours with Royalty but at opposite ends of the order of things. The old Talbot landlord taught me the ropes and seemed happy enough with my progress. Within days he left and the new landlord came and settled in. But it turned out that the new landlord had his own team of staff with him. I was no longer needed; I was just a pawn in their game. Surplus to requirements, I was given two weeks' notice.

Unsettled and insecure I went to the house of the six Graduates who now lived in Peckham, South London. I guessed Jimmy wouldn't have refused my company for the odd night. But I'd become closer to Aaron in recent times and he was my good friend. He happily let me sleep over in his room with him.

After I'd been given my notice, I didn't want to sleep in my room at the pub. Aaron was happy for me to stay with him in his room and we chatted and chatted like we'd done before. For two weeks Aaron and I slept together in his bed and I travelled back and forth every day to the Talbot. Only now we were not like brother and sister and we were more than just friends.

The six graduates had kept in touch with some of the other tenants who'd come and gone during our time at the Edwardian house. One called Marvin visited the Peckham house one evening while I was there. He wanted to take a summer trip to France. Although small and introverted, he seemed a nice enough person and I'd always wanted to travel. So, when he suggested that at the end of my employment, we should go backpacking together I thought, why not? I assumed he meant as friends.

My brief employment at the public house had ended and my newly purchased blue ruck-sack was packed. The battered old orange suitcase had done its time and with a broken latch, took a swift exit from my life. I fitted everything I owned into my ruck-sack and onto the train to Paris. Aaron let me borrow his blue and black, hand knitted jumper and I promised I would take good care of it. I felt close to him through it. I had no idea how long I would stay in France.

After a few days in Paris, my friend Marvin and I took a six-hour train journey to Morlaix in Brittany, a beautiful lush-green part of northern France. We carried heavy camping equipment and camped out in fields. We could only ask for a 'sandwich au fromage' in French so that's what we lived on. As it rained repeatedly, we tired easily. On top of the terrible weather, I couldn't enjoy traveling while knowing there was no place to come home to and I couldn't relax.

It turned out that the shy Marvin had a thing for me and he soon made his intentions clear. As I didn't have the same feelings for him, I couldn't bear being stuck in a tent with him. Our close proximity became an annoyance and we started to irritate one another so I left him in Morlaix and took the train back to Paris alone.

I was emotionally and literally totally lost in Paris. I had to rely on the sympathy of French strangers to get me back on the train to the international port and point me in the direction of England. My belongings weighed heavily on my back as I walked up the ramp onto the huge ferry. And she set sail. I felt a kind of numbness as I crossed the sea and the white cliffs of Dover increased their size. My homeland?

On arrival, in England, it crossed my mind that I should go back to Worcester instead of London. I was now over the age of 18 so perhaps I could get a council flat there now? But no, I wouldn't be able to even have my name listed on the waiting list as I now couldn't prove I was resident in Worcester. I'd been away living in London for over two years so I couldn't prove addresses in Worcester. I thought about trying to get a council flat in the Crystal Palace area where (not including Ben's address or the squats) I could prove at least 18 months of residence. But everyone knew that only pregnant girls would be helped.

So, with nowhere to go, I turned up at the house of the six graduates in Peckham, London. I was looking forward to seeing them all, especially Aaron. Still wearing his jumper I was in for a shock. While I'd been away, for less than a month, Aaron had been sleeping with another girl and now she was pregnant and a child was on its way. It was not at all in Aaron's plan and he was shocked but he'd accepted the situation like a true gentleman. He would be loyal to his new girl.

With a heavy heart I gave back Aaron's jumper. He didn't owe me any explanation as I'd never officially been his girlfriend and anyway, I'd been camping with Marvin in France which must have looked to everyone like we were at it. I felt no resentment towards Aaron, just more disappointment.

For several nights, in September, I slept in bed with Marty but, other than a hug, he did not attempt to touch me. He'd accepted that we were only friends and nothing more. He was such a good guy and I was such a fool. My twentieth birthday passed in the Peckham house. I said goodbye to my teenage years as I consumed a lot of lager. That was the last birthday I spent with those good friends.

There were no spare rooms at the Peckham house even though the Queen Bee had two, one small bedroom and a small workroom for her sewing machine and fashion materials. Marty and the boys gingerly suggested I might have her sewing room if she would agree to move the stuff from her 'workroom' into her bedroom. Like this she would save fifty per cent on her rent and I would be responsible for it instead. Queen bee was immediately threatened by this suggestion and the worker boy bees instantly backed off. I couldn't blame her; she needed her space and her determination to make it in London's fashion industry. The disagreeable tend to do well in this world.

It was unfair of me to continue squeezing in with Marty. I needed to find another place to stay. Marty had heard of a guy called Conrad who'd somehow managed to get himself a housing association flat in Penge, on the other side of Crystal Palace. Further out from central London. I'd met him once or twice before as he'd visited us all at number 11. He had black greasy hair, smoked a lot of weed and generally turned up at the student house on party nights.

I'd not taken much notice of Conrad when I'd been introduced. Now I needed to befriend him so I went off to find him and to suggest I have a room in his flat. I guess you could say that I was lucky as without hesitation, Conrad agreed that I could share his flat and share the very reasonably priced rent.

I hadn't worked since leaving the Talbot. The only thing I knew I could do for sure was working in McDonald's in Crystal Palace. It'd been two years since I'd worked there. Penge was close enough to get there with just a few stops on one bus. Of course, I'd never intended to work there again. Since I'd left, the general manger had changed and most of the staff had changed too. There was only one guy that I knew from when I'd worked there before and he was one of the lower managers called Chris. He vouched for me and I was offered to start work straightaway.

I moved my bags into Conrad's flat; I had my own unfurnished room which luckily already had a mattress on the floor. The next day I started back at McDonald's. But I was not alright. I felt very down in myself. It was now October and Winter was coming again and I had no heating in my room. I started a fire up in the open fireplace and the lady in the flat above us came and banged on the door. Screaming at me that the smoke had gone into her living room through the unmaintained chimney and I was not to light a fire again. I did not.

I was still smoking cigarettes and I wasn't taking care of myself at all. We had no cooking facilities other than Conrad's electric kettle, as the flat was still new to him and came completely unfurnished. I didn't want to buy anything such as an electric ring or pots and pans (even if I could afford them) as I would just have more things to carry if and when I inevitably moved again.

I lived on free burgers and chips at work and smoked like a trooper. By the time the cold weather came in I was sick with a chest infection. I'd always had a weak chest and scars on my lung from when I'd had pneumonias a child. It was not surprising that during my third winter as a smoker I was taken down.

Feeling despondent, by Christmas I lay down and just got to a point when I didn't want to get up again. I hardly moved and didn't go to work for two days and on the third day, unbelievably, Chris turned up to check up on me. He'd become concerned when there'd been no sign of me at work. He'd gone through my recent application pack and looked up my current address. Then, with another female lower-manager, he located the flat where I lay. My flat-mate Conrad had let them in and they took one look at me in the unheated place and decided I was suffering from, bronchitis, hyperthermia and depression. They went out to the shop and bought me cough medicine, cup-a-soups and pot-

noodles, as the only kitchen appliance available was a kettle, these items were the only hot meal substitutes possible.

Next day, Chris came back alone and he had a small electric heater with him. He'd borrowed it from his mother and I could keep it for the time being. Considering I only knew him as a manager, at my place of work, he was very kind to me. I think he was a Christian. There must be one person in every million people that turn out to be angels. They turn up when you least expect them and they help without reason, without expecting something in return. Chris was one in a million.

With boiling water, from the kettle, I prepared the cup-a-soups and pot-noodles and forced myself to eat them as well as taking the cough medicine. I made good use of the little heater that'd been lent to me. Whilst trying to get over the illness I thought about the kindness Chris had shown me and it gave me a little impetus to recover. Within a few more days I was back at work.

On Chris's insistence I'd been to see a doctor and had been diagnosed with bronchitis, iron deficiency and clinical depression. I'd been given medication for my chest infection and it slowly improved. Regular iron tablets eventually improved my physical strength. But other than causing a kind of numbness, the anti-depressants that the doctor gave me, didn't help. I was referred to a psychotherapist but found therapy to be of little use either. I carried on working anyway.

I didn't really know Conrad that well but as we were flat mates, I thought we ought to be friendly. So, one evening I went to chat with him in his room. I was used to hanging out in the boys' bedrooms at the student house so I thought little of it. He poured us a glass of wine each as we sat on his bed together watching his television. The evening went on and we chatted and enjoyed each other's conversation. Then suddenly, out of the blue, he lunged at me with the clear intention of planting a kiss and more! By reflex, I pushed him away and jumped up in absolute horror and disgust. I had no interest in him other than being flat mates. I had not even thought about him being male or how it might have looked that I was sitting in his bedroom drinking wine with him.

Conrad's notion that we might get it on, repulsed me! I was instantly nauseated by him and his greasy black hair. My shock and distaste, to his sudden advances, must have been written all over my face as I grimaced in shock. He was deeply offended by my reaction and angry with me for 'Leading him on.'

I guess I'd been led into a false sense of security with the male students/now graduates. None of them had ever lunged at me without clear encouragement. I felt like an idiot! I must have been still innocent or stupid. The natively of me sitting on Conrad's bed, drinking wine all evening and then being shocked at him for assuming I was interested. It's mind boggling. Having been raised in a family of females I still didn't know much about males or what effect my behaviour had on them. I just didn't understand them at all.

As the following days passed, I felt more embarrassed and cringed at the thought of Conrad's advances. After years of being an inconvenience to everyone, I became convinced that he wanted me out. I avoided bumping into him and quietly stayed in my own room as much as possible. When we bumped into each other in the kitchen, I said 'Hi' but he didn't reply. It was Conrad's flat and I knew he could make me leave at any minute. I wanted to get out before he threw me out.

I tried to think of what to do next. When I called Marty, I discovered that Jimmy had moved out of the Peckham house and some other friend had taken his room. If the graduates would have known how unhappy I was at Conrad's, I'm sure they would have offered the room to me. But there was no telephone at Conrad's flat and they had no way of contacting me. I got Jimmy's new address and telephone number from Marty.

Jimmy was now living with an old friend and conveniently, his new place was also in Penge. We were still friends, of a kind, so I went to see him. Over the coming days and weeks, I visited and often stayed-over with him. Of course, I became more notches on his bedpost. But I knew that, in his own way, Jimmy did care for me. But I couldn't move in with him, at his mate's flat. And we still weren't exactly 'a couple - we never would be.

Nonetheless, I stayed over often, partly because I loved being with Jimmy and partly to avoid the cold atmosphere of Conrad's flat. But I was wasting time and putting off the inevitable. I needed to find somewhere else to live. I didn't want to become a nuisance by turning up all desperate again at the Graduates' house. I'd completely lost contact with Anna but had managed to remain friends with Vicky. I went to find her to plead for help.

CHAPTER 11

Yogi

Vicky's council flat hadn't worked out so well. She'd been given a place on a very rough council estate in a run-down area in south-east London. She was no longer with her boyfriend. She felt threatened by the gangs of youths hanging around on the estate and felt nervous going in and out of the block. She was already considering the possibility of being transferred to another area. When one night she came home from work and found she too had been burgled. She felt afraid for her own safety, packed up as much as she could carry and left almost immediately.

The typing course, that Vicky had attended, was sponsored by the Greater London council. The award for the best student was employment in County Hall, central London. Vicky had always been a clever girl and she already had a string of school leaving certificates from grammar school.

To top this, she came first in the typing course and was now working as an apprentice in County Hall. As a young employee, she'd been given day-release from work to attend further education college. She was now at the age when she would have to pay to study A levels but the fees were covered by her employer. She was also working parttime, in the evenings, in a public house called the Fox on the Hill. This pub was located in another area of south east London known as Herne Hill. There, she'd made friends with several of the mostly male punters.

On the evening of the burglary, she'd fled from the rough council flat and rushed to the Fox on the Hill, where she knew many people. One of them was a funny little middle-aged man, and possibly an alcoholic, nick-named Yogi. He owned a three bedroomed terrace house nearby. He lived alone having recently separated from his wife and boy-child. He was keen on Vicky and suggested she vacate her council flat and come and stay with him instead - for free. She'd already taken him up on this offer.

I turned up at the pub and chatted with Vicky as she worked behind the bar. I told her how desperately unhappy I was at Conrad's place and she came up with a plan. She would talk to Yogi and somehow convince him to let me have a room in his house too. Vicky was very convincing when she wanted to be and I was quietly confident that she'd do a good job.

Vicky did a great job and Yogi agreed that I could have his box-room for fifteen pounds per week, inclusive of bills! This was a good deal and I jumped at the chance to move from Conrad's flat and into a fully furnished, heated house with cooking facilities and hot water and all the things that people are accustomed to having in the Western world.

From Yogi's house it was a bit of a trek to work for me but I managed to get there on the busses. I didn't like working at MacDonald's the second time around and I felt it was a road to nowhere but at least I had a job and I could pay my rent. I regularly went to the Fox on the Hill, where Vicky worked and I got to know many of the regulars there too.

Vicky introduced me to a mixed-race guy named Vince. She'd actually known him from primary school and she'd re-established contact again, at the pub, by pure chance. Vince and I hit it off straight away. I guess we were similar in character, both a bit over-excitable and both a bit hyper. But I'd say that Vince was more hyper than I was, I'd say that he was a bit wild!

Vince had a motorbike and he'd often take me out on it. He went way too fast for my liking. I was always a bit of a scaredy-cat. We'd usually end up back at the pub where we'd play pinball. Vince was pretty good at it, I guess he'd spent a lot of time practising. He was one of the funniest, nicest guys I ever met. He was also very intelligent although he did a good job of acting the fool and hiding it.

Vince lived at home, locally, with his parents and he used to sneak me into his bedroom which was full of musical instruments including a full drum kit! He took it upon himself to teach me to play the drums. Well, he must have had the patience of a saint. And his listening parents must have thought he'd regressed somewhat. He was a skilled and accomplished drummer at just nineteen years of age. A multi-talented guy, going places. I always looked forwards to seeing Vince, he was an absolute breath of fresh air.

It felt luxurious for me to live in a normal house with a television and a living room. I appreciated it and always made sure I gave Yogi his rent money on the day it was due. I cleaned up after myself and often spent my time off, trying my best to do housework. I didn't want to be thrown out for bad behaviour or from lack of doing housework or late rent or any of a number of possible reasons that one can be expelled for.

Vicky didn't have to pay rent or do any housework because Yogi was obsessed with her. But that really didn't bother me, I was just thankful to her for convincing him to let me stay. She'd done me a great favour. It was obvious Yogi was crazy about Vicky. He was punching well above his weight and he knew it. He didn't seem to mind that she was obviously using him for free accommodation and she did no housework and never picked up anything after herself. She was obviously taking advantage of him but he seemed happy and I didn't mind either, it seemed a good enough deal for everyone concerned. We were three adults and if we were all happy with the arrangement, then it was no one else's business. But I was anxious that one day Yogi might get fed up with the situation and I knew where that would leave me. So, I did my best to keep a nice atmosphere, by doing housework.

Yogi never seemed to tire of Vicky's deportment. Something else happened to get us thrown out. I was on my way back home from work one afternoon and Yogi was running up the street towards me in a state of frenzy.

'You can't go in Jen!' Yogi spoke breathlessly. His obvious state of panic told me something was very wrong.

'What d'ya mean, what's happened?' My tone was immediately abrupt and nervous.

'She's back, she's in the house, you can't go in!' He continued.

At first, I felt confused as I thought he was talking about Vicky. Then the penny dropped. 'You mean your wife came back?!' I felt a wave of fear and shock as my words came out and my legs went weak.

'I'm sorry mate, you can't go in there, she's going mental' Yogi stood staring at me for a few seconds and then he turned on his heels and ran towards the front door of his house.

'What we gonna do? Where we gonna go? What about our stuff? I called after him.

He stopped in his tracks, 'I dunno mate, just find Vicky and make sure she don't turn up ere, I don't want no trouble. You've got me number, just call me and I'll work out a way to get you ya stuff'

I stood in the middle of the street, shaking my head and taking deep breaths. Then I slowly turned and walked in the direction of the Fox on the Hill. I hoped Vicky would come straight there from her daytime job, before going home. Home? Well we couldn't call it that anymore.

When Vicky arrived, she was all smiles. 'Alright, whatcha doing ere so early?' She started.

'Yogi's wife's back, she's at the house now. We can't live there anymore, we can't go back and I don't even know if we can get our stuff out!' I blurted out without taking a breath.

'On shit' Vicky said, as her big, brown eyes widened and her face went pale.

We pulled up two stools at the bar and ordered two Bacardi and Cokes. We sat there for a while with our heads in our hands as we leant on the bar.

'I hate this life Vicky, I can't stand it, it's just so shit - all the time, I just don't know what to do to make it better.' My voice was starting to crack.

Vicky was a lot more resourceful than I was. By now, I'd lost almost all hope and was living on empty. 'Let me fink,' She went quiet for moment, 'Look there's only one guy I know that might be able to help us, his name's Den, he lives in the East End, he's got his own house and he rents out rooms. I dunno if he's got any spare rooms though but I'll give him a call.'

'Where's the east end?' I questioned

'Whatcha mean, where's the east end? It's in east London innit, don'tcha bloody know anyfink, jeez youre just a little lost lamb ain't ya!' Vicky rolled her eyes and breathed out in a kind of defeat before muttering, 'bloody farmers'

I just shrugged my shoulders and then nodded in a kind of hopeless agreement as Vicky started to gather five pence pieces up from her purse. I put my hand in my pocket and handed over a couple of coins. With our collection, we made our way to the local telephone box. It stank of stale urine which was usual but at least the telephone was working. It was never guaranteed.

Vicky dialled the number and pushed a five pence piece in. Next, she was chatting with Den. The full charm offensive. She sounded as if she didn't have a care in the world. Didn't want to sound desperate she'd said to me afterwards. She did a great job. But Den didn't have any spare rooms available.

As we two, twenty-year-old orphan-girls, stood in

the stale urine of that south London telephone box with no home to go to, I begged and pleaded, in my head, for someone to help us.

'Awwwer, help, I just can't, oh, I can't take anymore Vick! Help, help, help!' I was starting to talk gibberish and bordering on hysterical.

Vicky held me tight as she did her best to reassure me. It must have taken every bit of strength she had left to hold back her own tears. 'We'll be ok Jen, we'll sort somefing out'

'Lesbians!' Someone shouted as they passed us in the phone box.

'Oh Jeez.' I said, as I rolled my teary eyes.

Vicky started laughing and I managed to muster up a smile.

'I'm gonna call Den again,' Vicky had a look of determination in her watery eyes.

'Hello Den, it's Vicky again. Look, we've literally got nowhere ta go Den. Is there any chance we can just stay in ya living room, just for a few nights, just til we sort somefing else out, I'm begging ya Den, please can you elp us!?' 'Oh, fank God.' Vicky said as she sighed a breath of relief and replaced the telephone receiver. 'We can stay with Den for a few days at least. Oh, fank God. I was worried we were gonna sleep in the park tonight'

'Oh, thank God for this Den, whoever he is' I said, as a kind of hesitant relief came over me. 'Thought ya didn't wanna sound desperate though?' I had a cheeky smile on my face as I tried to hide my resent distress.

'Well, needs must, I guess' Vicky replied, as we both tried to laugh at the absurdity of our lives.

Once I saw a wasp enter a guy's bottle of coke. The bloke obviously hated wasps and so he put a beer-mat over the top of the bottle and shook the bottle vigorously. The wasp was clearly delirious on his few seconds of respite in between violent shakes.

I told the guy, 'Stop it! Either let the creature go or kill it, stop this torture! But the guy insisted on continuing the shaking.

For some reason I thought about that wasp. He'd only gone with his instinct, innocently looking for sugar and he'd inadvertently trespassed into someone's fizzy drink. That guy's hand was like the hand of God, with all the power, he intermittently shook the wasp to near death. The wasp had no control, no hope and must have felt so sick (if wasps can feel sick) while awaiting his eventual fate. I felt my life was like that. I felt ill, I felt that life was punishing me, torturing me. I was getting thrown around like that wasp. Now and then I'd be allowed a little respite only to return to the robust and cruel shaking by the hand of God.

After Vicky had noted our new temporary address in the East End, she'd passed the phone to me to call Yogi. She was so angry with him and didn't want to hear his voice ever again. Any affection Vicky ever had for Yogi, had already turned to pure hate. So, I was the one who needed to make the arrangements to collect our belongings.

Yogi said his wife had popped out to visit her mother and now was a good time to grab our stuff from his house. We must move quickly as bumping into her could turn nasty. I said we'd be there within half an hour and we'd have to call a cab to get there that quickly.

We were running out of coins and only had one left to call the taxi cab. We got the number off the wall, inside the telephone box. A card stuck up next to the many cards with naked photographs of prostitutes and adverts for jobs in peep-shows. I remembered when someone had suggested Vicky and I could earn good money selling ourselves and I wondered if it would have been an easier life than what we'd so far opted for.

The cab picked us up fifteen minutes later and took us to Yogi's house. He looked sheepish while he waited for us to get our belongings out of his place. I was well practised at moving out of my accommodation quickly. I just literally chucked everything into my rucksack and any leftovers went into the carrier bags. No messing, I was ready to go in five minutes flat. But in comparison to me, Vicky was taking her time.

'Come on Vick! Yogi's misses is gonna catch us if we

don't hurry up, you know she's crazy, come on, let's go!' I stressed.

'I don't give a shit, innit' Vicky replied and I believed she really had gone passed caring.

Another five minutes and we were both ready to leave.

'I'm sorry Vick, sorry Jen.' Yogi said, as we were on our way out of the front door.

'It's alright Yogi, it's not your fault' I replied.

'Where you gonna go?' Yogi continued.

'The East End.' Vicky said coldly.

'You will be back though yeah? You don't wanna stay East, it's rough as fuck over that end. We'll still see you in the pub yeah?' Yogi was sounding a little pathetic.

I managed to force a smile and a half nod of the head. We certainly intended to come back to south London. The East End meant nothing to me. I'd gotten to know my way around a lot of the south so that area meant much more. And I definitely planned on seeing Vince again. Anyway, this Den couldn't help us out for long and so I assumed we would definitely make it back to the south side in a short time. Within a week. That's what I hoped for. But I never lived in South London again and poor Vince never knew where I disappeared to. He never heard from me or saw me again.

CHAPTER 12

East End

Stratford - East London was way too far away for me to go to work from. If I'd attempted to continue working at McDonald's in Crystal Palace it would have taken an hour and a half each way at least. I guess I could have transferred to a nearer one but it wasn't a great job for me anyway. So now I needed to find a new job and somewhere to live. It was such a worry being without a permanent home and without a job. A feeling you'd think I'd be accustomed to by now. But I never got used to it.

I took the underground train to central London and registered with several agencies for potential office work. This seemed to be a step in the right direction for me. Vicky and I also spent a lot of time searching for accommodation in newspapers to try to get back to South East London. We spent good money on a deposit for a flat that didn't even exist via a fake housing agency. It is easy for the unscrupulous to take from the desperate.

In the end, Den realised that he would either have to throw us out on the street or let us rent the living room and luckily for us the latter applied. It was a small unfurnished room so we went out and bought ourselves bunk beds to take up less space and we went halves. Den lent us the money and added what we owed him onto the weekly rent payments.

Including Den, there were four guys living in the house. They were all around ten years older than us and all single. They all worked and spent their evenings at the local pub. None of these guys had any interest in marriage or the prospect of having children. If Vicky or I had made a move on any of them, I'm sure they wouldn't have said no. But none of them could even be bothered to make a move on us which suited us fine. I guess you could call them 'drop-outs from society,' they all had drink problems, at the very least. But they were intelligent, funny and friendly enough.

Vicky and I now had our room which we left clean but very untidy. The rest of the house was a filthy mess but I was not going to complain about that. There was a home telephone number and I could give that out to the office agencies as I registered with them for work.

Vicky and I started to socialise at the local public house which was called the King Edward and nick-named the Eddie. If Den and his friends weren't at work or in the house, you'd always find them in the Eddie. We frequented there several nights of the week. In those days men would generally buy girls or women drinks. We regularly drank more alcohol than we could manage and being drunk or feeling sick from a serious hangover became normality to us and all the other tenants of the Stratford house.

After a week or two in Stratford I received a call from an agency offering me a temporary job in the Lloyds bank building, in the city of London. They needed a temporary tea lady as the usual one was having a week's holiday. At the age of twenty I felt very young to be a tea lady but a job was a job. For a week, I was there boiling a huge tank for the water every day. Then I'd load it all up on the trolly ready to go up and down on the lift. I'd lug the trolly around the offices, serving teas, coffees and biscuits. I was terrible at it. Even a simple job of serving tea, takes time to master and by the time I'd started to get the hang of it, I was no longer needed. This is a good way to make yourself feel useless.

Most of the staff had looked down their noses at me but one or two were friendly even suggesting that I ought to be working in the office rather than being a tea lady. It made me think that maybe I could work in an office. Most of the females didn't look that different to me other than the way they dressed in their expensive skirt suits and blouses. But I assumed they were cleverer than me or at least they had a higher education.

The tea lady job came to an end and within a few days the agency called me again. This time they needed a temporary office clerk in a finance company in New Cavendish Street near Oxford Circus in central London. I was only put forward for this as, on my application, I'd mentioned my school leaving certificates that I'd taken at college. A minimum of five Ordinary levels were required for this temporary post including maths and English. I'd only scraped four O' levels which did not include maths so I lied on the application form. It was the only way of getting in somewhere. Luckily no-one asked to see my non-existent maths certificate or any of my other legitimate qualification certificates actually.

Back in the first year of my secondary school at the age of eleven, us children had been thrilled to have a very slack teacher called Mister Farmer. He'd been teaching at the school for more than thirty years and was sick to death of the place. He'd done his time with children that didn't want to learn and he was biding his time as retirement was just around the corner. The children in my year knew of Mister Farmer's reputation for letting kids mess around and showing them a thoroughly good time. We were not disappointed. From day one he told us that we were free to do whatever we wanted in class. We could even bring in board-games, to pass the time, if we liked.

The following year we were in big trouble as we were to be taught by Mister Wallace, a terrifyingly strict maths teacher. He was horrified by our lack of basic mathematic knowledge and vowed to whip us into shape during the second year. That was a stressful year as he tried in vain to educate us.

We were all relieved when we discovered that we were to again be with Mister Farmer in the third year. This was to be Mister Farmer's final year so if he got caught handing out cigarettes to the boys it wouldn't be the end of the world for him. He didn't exactly hand out the cigarettes, he just placed them down on a desk and said if he didn't see them being taken, while his back was turned, then it was nothing to do with him. He placed three Woodbine cigarettes down on a front desk and turned his back. Instantly a boy called Terry jumped up and grabbed the fags. He went straight out to the boy's toilets for a smoke. We kids thought Mister Farmer was pretty cool.

By the fourth year we were all hopeless cases. I doubt anyone of that class ever managed to reach an adult level of maths. At the time, Mister Farmer's 'maths sans maths' classes seemed hilarious but by the time of my first job in a finance office I realised it was not so funny.

On my first day, I made myself as smart as I could and took the central line underground train from Stratford to Oxford Circus. The tube was jam-packed at that time of day. Then a short walk along Regents Street and New Cavendish Street. I found the finance company and reported to the boss to let him know I'd arrived. I had not worked in an office before, except for being a tea lady, but I'd always enjoyed English at school and college. I got along well enough with my new office friends.

Quite a lot of maths was needed for this job and as I'd missed a lot of this subject at school, I knew I was going to struggle. With the use of a calculator (which I first needed to learn how to use for this complicated kind of maths) and a smile in the right places at the right time, I struggled but somehow managed to get by with some help from my new colleagues.

The people in the finance office seemed to like me even though they all realised, almost immediately, that my maths was not really up to scratch. I really had no right to work in 'accounts,' I couldn't even recognise big numbers, my education level was so poor. But I suppose my English and my communication skills somehow compensated. Although not really, as maths is pretty important in a finance office! My colleagues must have thought I was capable of learning though as someone put in a good word for me with the boss and I got taken on full time!

It was at this point that I decided to contact my uncle in Birmingham. I still remembered his telephone number off by heart. It was the first time he or any other, so-called family member, had heard from me in three years. No one had had sight or sound of me and knew not of my whereabouts or welfare.

'Where the hell have you been?' My auntie answered, as she realised it was me calling.

'I've been living in London, south London, Crystal Palace and other places but now I'm in East London.' I spoke.

'Well, we've been worried sick about you!' she continued, 'disappearing like that at the age of seventeen and not bothering to let us know your address! What were you thinking of! You could have at least let us know you're ok."

'Well, I'm letting you know now, innit,' I proceeded to recite my latest east London address and after giving the post-code my auntie burst out laughing.

'Ha, your accent has changed! You sound like a Cockney! Are you enjoying it down in London? I'll pass you over to your uncle'

A similar conversation continued with my uncle. They both talked to me with excitement in their voices as though I'd gone off to university, or something similar. A kind of denial of the truth I suppose. The truth being that not one of my relatives gave a damn about me. If they had, they'd have offered me a home. Or at least they'd have reported me missing when I'd disappeared.

I used to watch television programs about missing teenagers and felt jealous when their families cried out for them. My family never cried for me.

When I'd lived in Worcester at least a couple of teenage girls had been reported missing when they'd disappeared. They'd been taken by a sick and perverted couple who'd held them prisoners and tortured them to death but nobody knew at the time. I'd come dangerously close to being one of their victims. Their remains were found many years later in a cellar in one house and buried under a patio at another house. These girls had been reported missing and their details had been all over the West Midland's newspapers and even on the national news. Can you imagine, if I'd have been found, under the patio, people would say, 'Oh we didn't even realise she'd gone missing!'

'Are you enjoying London life?' My uncle continued, after having another chuckle about my new 'Cockney accent.'

I assumed the question was rhetorical and proceeded to reiterate my current address.

'You didn't report me missing to the police did ya?' I asked.

'No - I'll pass your address onto your sister and I

guess she'll let your father have it, bloody useless he is.' I didn't know what to reply to that. 'Oh, how funny, your accent has changed so much, you sound like a cockney now, are you enjoying it in London?'

CHAPTER 13

Breakdown

The next day the sun rose up in the sky and everything appeared to be the same as before. But although I looked the same in the mirror, I was not. Something had changed. A department had opened up in my mind that would never ever fully close again.

I prepared myself for my journey into central London and made my way to the underground station. The platform was always packed with other commuters at this time of day. As the train pulled up, everyone made hast and nudged themselves forward. We all knew this was the last stop on the line where any of us might be lucky enough to find a seat. The train was already crowded and would get progressively more packed as it made its way into the nucleus of the vast city. I didn't manage to get a seat and found myself standing up holding onto one of those dangly hanging handles. And then it happened.

The thought crossed my mind that I might faint. But that thought passed by so quickly that I had no chance to digest it. I suddenly wanted to get out of the train but by now it was deep underground again and heading towards the epicentre. My heart started to beat faster, so fast that I became breathless. The train started to slow down in the depths of the earth and I feared it would stop in between stations. I could think of only one thing, that I had to get out!

Tubes often paused in tunnels during rush hours and this day was no different. I became dizzy. I breathed deeper. I breathed quicker. My heart raced as I hyperventilated. I got progressively dizzier. My hands started to tremor. I looked at my hands. I became abnormally afraid for the situation. Literally Terrified. My emotions had gone out of sync to the current situation. I was completely overcome with alarm. 'I don't feel well' I said out loud, but no one took any notice. The ones closest to me just stared with glazed eyes as if still half asleep. Now I had drawn attention to myself and I felt embarrassed. My heart beat faster, so fast I could hear it beating in my ears and I couldn't catch my breath. I had black spots in front of my eyes. I wanted to get off the train but we were in a tunnel and I could not escape. I started to cry and without speaking, a man next to me passed me a paper tissue.

As the train pulled up at the next stop, I squeezed through the crowds to exit. I sat on the platform until I'd stopped shaking and I'd got my breath back. Ten minutes later and the following train was in. I was going to be late for work if I missed this one. So, I pushed my way through the crowds to get on. But as soon as the train pulled away, all the same symptoms immediately reappeared.

Somehow, I managed to stay on and get to Oxford Circus. Then a short walk to my place of work. There, I mulled over what was happening to me but I really didn't understand. Perhaps I had become claustrophobic?

After failing to balance the books three times, I handed the calculator over to my mentor. Then I muddled through the rest of the day in the account's office. I was dreading my return trip to Stratford. The journey would normally take only half an hour by tube train. But I would have to keep getting off to get my breath back when I felt ill, which was all of the time. So, it took me much longer to get home.

After that, every time I attempted the underground, I got the same apprehension. An indescribable feeling really but something similar to a sense of drowning. This was something so awful. And the only logical solution was to avoid the tube train altogether.

The bus was the only other option. But the bus

journey was a much more laborious one. With the abundance of vehicles at that time of day, I was stuck in almost continuous traffic jams. The journey to work would now take one and a half hours, each way, every day. Ridiculous, I know but I could not bring myself to attempt the underground anymore. I couldn't risk feeling that ill. I had to avoid it. But you can't run away from yourself, can you?

I had no understanding of what was happening to me. I continued to avoid the underground train but then the same symptoms caught up with me on the bus. I felt I couldn't breathe. I would get off the bus from time to time to try and get my breath back. Then I'd get back on. This continued. It was starting to take longer and longer for me to get into work and back from work. I got more and more exhausted.

With hindsight, I suppose it was some kind of a nervous disorder or a classic nervous breakdown. But I really didn't know what was going on. I had no one to talk to, no one to explain my condition. If only I'd have had someone around me that could tell me what was happening to me. Or a kindly relative who loved me and gave me somewhere to go to recuperated. But I suppose if I'd have been privileged to such refuge, I'd never have gotten into this state in the first place. Maybe with some rest and care, something like a rehabilitation centre, I could have gotten through it. But there was no nurturing place for me and I was caught in a downward spiral.

My office job was typically Monday to Friday so weekends became a welcome relief from the trauma of the journey. Come Friday evening I'd make my way to the Eddie for a couple of drinks to wind down. I could enter by myself as it was guaranteed that I'd find the company of either Vicky or at least one of the guys from the house there, propping up the bar.

I'd started to make other friends at the pub too. One of them was a local east-ender named Mark. And I guess he was the one 'waiting in the wings for me.' He was twenty, the same age as me. He'd lived in east London all of his life. He was a bit of a punk-rocker in a time when the punk era was really already over.

Mark had two tattoos, one on each arm. On his right arm was an eagle but the head of the bird was slightly out of proportion and a little too small for the body. His left arm showed the name of his favourite lager which should have read 'Tennent's.' But the tattooist had made a mistake and spelled it 'tenants' as in a person who occupies land or property from a landlord, a tenant who rents a flat! Mark had pointed out the errors in both of his tattoos with good humour. He seemed to be able to laugh at himself. I found that to be an attractive quality. He was a member of an organisation that I'd never heard of - the Animal Liberation Front. And he was a strict vegetarian. He had a strong and true cockney accent and a confidence that came from having knowledge of his area. He knew his way around and he belonged in the east End. I envied and admired that and wished I belonged somewhere like he did.

East London was where I was now so if I could feel safe with Mark, that sense of belonging was surely going to be a good thing. He intrigued me. He was not bad looking with his almost black hair and soft blue eyes and he had a certain cockney charm about him. I needed someone to make me feel at home in this new neck of the woods. I wanted to love someone. He was most definitely interested in being with me. We joked and flirted together. We played pool and I won and we laughed. When I put money in the duke box, he came up behind me and put his arms around me.

'Wha ya gonna pu' on?' He spoke.

'I dunno, erm, Frankie Goes to Hollywood, The Power of Love?'

'Nah, that's crap, put Simple Minds on, Don't You Forget about me'

'ok'

'Don't you try and pretend,'

'It's my feeling we'll win in the end,'

'I won't harm you or touch your defences,'

'Vanity and insecurity ah'

'Don't you forget about me,'

'Don't, don't, don't, don't,'

'Don't you forget about me'

I befriended girls at the Eddie too. Linda and Annie were best friends like me and Vicky. Linda was a student at the local polytechnic. Annie was a little older and had recently graduated with a degree in sociology. She was doing well and had landed herself a job as a social-worker at the local Saint Andrew's hospital. Student Linda was my favourite of the two; she was more attractive and friendly while Annie was dumpy, plain and standoffish. She rarely spoke and always avoided eye contact with me. Having once had a bad experience with a hospital social worker I was unimpressed with Annie's new employment and I had a natural wariness of her.

CHAPTER 14

Family

My uncle had passed on my new east London address to my sister, who'd given it to my father and I now had re-established written communication with all of my 'family' but I saw little point in it. They were my blood but I knew for sure that they would never help me in times of trouble. That seemed guaranteed. I never really understood why they even wanted contact with me. Perhaps they just wanted to hear of my stories of my struggles to survive. Well, I had no intention of telling them anything. But once I'd entered into letter writing with them, I felt strangely and ridiculously obligated to keep it up.

In many ways I regretted re-establishing contact. I was now stuck in a fake relationship with family members who'd not helped me or even reported me missing when I'd disappeared. If I tried to question them about the days when they'd abandoned me back in Worcester, they'd just get defensive and accuse me of being a troublesome teenager. Within a few months my father had defended himself by calling me a thief and a liar and I dropped all contact with him. I continued on with what I called a Christmas card relationship with my sister and uncle. Afraid to broach the painful subject of my rejection by them anymore, I kept contact to a minimal.

I was still struggling with some kind of nervous condition and finding it difficult to get in and out of central London by public transport. Getting to work by avoiding the underground train was like a marathon event. But I was doing my best and putting my past to the back of my mind as much as possible. I had a new distraction now and I threw myself into my relationship with Mark and his Cockney family. I suppose I was eager to fall in love and to be loved and as on previous liaisons I'd thrown patience and caution to the wind.

Mark and his two brothers were close in age at twenty, nineteen and eighteen. The three of them looked up to the notorious Cray twin gangsters. They idolised them. The Crays had been famous for their violent reign of terror in east London back in the 1960s. Although now they were languishing in separate high security prisons. Mark and his brothers liked to think of themselves as kind of similar to the Cray twins. It was a bit of a joke that they now fantasised about ruling the east end.

I met Mark's Mother and I admired how the boys respected her. I suppose people would say that Mark was a 'mummy's boy' but I only thought of this as a positive thing. The bond they all shared was something I hoped to be a part of. I got on well with them all and felt I was becoming one of them within a short space of time.

The brothers were all regulars at the Eddie. On occasion an alcohol fuelled fight would break out. One of the brothers and one or two unsuspecting brawlers would suddenly find out that they'd taken on not one but three brothers all at once. The brothers often deliberately caused trouble and then backed each other up, no matter what. That's when I learned that when you glass someone you don't have to waste time breaking the glass to show the jagged edges first (as they do in the movies) Rather the whole glass just goes straight into the face and that's where it breaks. It's a horrible thing to witness.

Although I didn't agree with the violence, I was in awe of how the brothers supported one another. Mark seemed like he would lay his life down if anyone even verbally disrespected one of his family members and his family would do the same for him. I longed for that kind of loyalty and security and I attached myself to them in the hope that I would be protected and loved with the same intensity. Added to this potential loyalty, Mark was forthcoming about wanting to have a baby with me. Well, I guess that was the music to my ears I'd been waiting for.

Mark had moved out from the family home and was subletting a ground floor flat on a busy main road in an area further out to the east from central London, called Manor Park. It was a housing association flat, the bottom half of a mid-terrace house that was not really in a liveable condition. There was no bathroom, just an outdoor toilet leftover from Victorian times. As compensation there was a shower cubicle in the corner of the kitchen but it was not usable, no longer connected to water supply. But that was not a problem as Mark would shower back at him mum's house when required.

Mark's flat was not in a liveable condition but for a young working man aged twenty, it did the job. Mark was out all day during the week days, working as a trainee car mechanic. As he finished work, he would go to his mother's house for dinner and a bath and then he would generally go to the Eddie in Stratford. So the flat was really just a place to lay his head and keep his stuff and have a coffee. It was like a half-way to independence place with a fall-back option of his mother a couple of miles away. Practise playing at adulthood so to speak.

The official tenant of Mark's place was a friend of his. For a short while they'd lived there together, then his friend had moved away and Mark had continued to live there alone. Therefore, Mark was illegally subletting but that wasn't really a problem. If he got found out and thrown out, he knew he could always go back to his mum's.

The condition of the flat was not in an acceptable order by any stretch of the imagination but as Mark was subletting, he couldn't really complain about it. So instead, he'd decided not to pay the rent to the housing association, saving himself money. As he didn't pay the rent it was impossible to complain about the ill state of the place or to have the association do any repairs.

A colony of small mice would make their way into Mark's flat in the still of the night. This didn't bother Mark as he said he 'preferred animals to humans' He actually would put a few crisps down on his bedroom floor to feed the little blighters and sometimes stay awake to watch them munching on their feast. I thought this was odd and perhaps not the best cause of action but it was his choice if he wanted to invite the wildlife in to share with him.

I was still living in the Stratford house and sharing a room with Vicky but it was never really a permanent home and we knew we could be out on our arses at short notice. As I'd thrown myself into a relationship with Mark and things were moving quickly I often preferred to spend the night with him. So as the pub closed we would go back on the bus to his place in Manor Park.

There was a double bed and a rented colour television that needed fifty pence pieces in the slot at the back for it to work. A fifty pence piece would enable us to watch television for a few hours and then it would cut out until we put another coin in the back. The place was a hovel but I was blinded by my affection for Mark. Anyway, I'd lived in worse places and Den's place was not much better.

Praying for the best at the age of twenty I still had hope in my heart for my future. I was eager to be part of a Mark's family and to have a family of my own. I was swept away by the first throws of passion and my head was in the clouds. I threw myself into a physical and emotional relationship and there were moments of great fun. But I was still getting ill on my way into work every day. In fact I was feeling much worse to the point where I felt terribly nauseous. What I believed must be claustrophobia, was bringing me down so I turned to Mark for comfort.

'You alright babe? Mark enquired. I'd had a particularly difficult journey home from work and by the time I got to the Manor Park flat I felt sick and faint. 'You ain't pregnant are ya?'

This possibility had already crossed my mind, 'Well I could be, how'd you feel about it?'

'I want a baby, you know I do!' he continued. He looked happy enough.

'Yeah, but we're only twenty and we haven't got a proper place to live!' I spoke.

'Twenty's old enough and we'll both be twenty-one by the time the baby's born. The council will give us a proper flat then and any other problems and Mum will help us out, she loves babies.' He insisted.

A few days later I managed to get an appointment with a local doctor and I did a pregnancy test there. A few days after that a positive test confirmed that I was expecting. Mark seemed much more confident about the whole situation than I was. We'd only known each other for a couple of months but he seemed adamant that this baby was meant to be.

I was still officially sharing the bunk beds in a room with Vicky but I was spending less time there and more time at Mark's place. But I spent the evening of the positive test result back with Vicky and she was shocked to hear my news.

'Get rid of it, that's my advice.' She said, without hesitation. 'You're too young and you ain't known Mark long enough and to be honest, although I do like him and I can see what you see in him well - he seems to be a bit of a nutter,' Vicky had grown quite forthright and hard from her difficult life. She'd had a tough time and now she had a straightforward, no-nonsense character. Which was strange as I seemed to grown softer and weaker from my difficult life. I suppose trauma effects people differently. She was telling me straight-up what she would do if she was me. But she was not me. 'Your life's over once you've got a kid you know! You don't wanna be stuck indoors changing nappies, do you?!'

I felt so ill that I couldn't even think straight. This, all day, morning sickness was something else, I had no idea it could be so bad. I knew that Vicky cared about me but she was talking from her own perspective. She still had big plans for her own life. While my big dreams had passed me by and now the thought of having a child and doing all I could for their life, was good enough for me. I felt useless but I could still be a good mum. I would now at least have justification for my existence.

The following evening, Vicky helped me to pack up my belongings from our shared room. Now she realised I was planning on going ahead with the baby she offered her congratulations and even started to get excited for me.

'I do like Mark ya know? He's alright, he's not stupid, he's actually quite intelligent. It's just all this 'Animal Liberation Front' stuff and the 'Meat Means Murder' stuff he keeps going on about' Vicky said as she rolled her eyes.

'I know, he's quite passionate about it all ya know? He says he's an anarchist and an activist. But the only action I've ever seen him take is talking about it all with a pint of lager in his hand.' I smiled at the thought and we both started laughing. 'Ha ha he is a vegetarian though!' I finished off. I don't know why we found this all so funny.

That evening I struggled to move house on the bus from Stratford to Manor Park, it was a half an hour journey of stopping and starting in traffic. I now had more stuff than I could manage in one trip so I needed to do the trip back twice.

CHAPTER 15

Manor Park Mark

A couple of months past and I continued to struggle from the far side of east London into London's West end by avoiding the underground train. I still didn't understand what was happening. The busses from Manor Park to Oxford circus would take around two hours each way, each day. The bus constantly stopped and started to let people on and off and it was slow and full of fumes because of the rush-hour traffic. And rush-hour in London is more like three hours. I felt terribly sick and on occasion got off to throw up. By the time I got to my office job I was usually good for nothing and on occasion they even sent me home.

Back at Mark's flat I tried to make the place as homely as I could. We lived in the back room which was a double bedroom. My pale blue, pattered quilt covered the bed and the television rested directly at its foot. Mark's hi fi record player was on the left and the bed was pushed up against the wall on the right hand side which was my side. There was a back door off our bedroom which went straight out to the toilet and the back yard that was full of overgrown grasses and weeds. The floor was covered in dirty green lino.

As there was no bathroom, a shower cubical was housed in the corner of the kitchen. This was a strange thing to see in a kitchen but I guess, needs must. Unfortunately the actual shower had been ripped out of the cubical exposing electric wiring so no washing facilities were available at all. There were two electric rings on the stove so that was something at least. I tried to cook but Mark didn't like the smell of meat so I cut it out of my diet. I managed to make some weird vegetarian pasta concoctions instead.

A few weeks passed and by three months pregnant I was already starting to show. I put it down to my skinniness and the bump popping out more on thin girls. I thought I'd have had another few weeks before my condition was apparent to everyone but it appeared I was showing early and the sickness continued.

One morning I was struggling to prepare myself for the arduous journey to work when I felt something move down below. Mark had already left for the day as I went to the toilet and noticed something amiss. I got stressed immediately. Things were not right. I grabbed my bag and walked down to the nearest telephone box which was under the noisy Ilford flyover. I dialled one of the taxi cab numbers that was up on the wall and soon enough I was in Newham general hospital.

'A threatened miscarriage' they said. I managed to get a message to Mark as I knew his mum's telephone number. He visited her most days so he soon got the message. Later that day he came to visit me at the hospital.

The following day I was booked in for a scan. 'Well, well, well,' Said the scanning lady. But she wasn't giving much away.

Back on the ward and the team of specialists were doing their rounds. I sat up straight for their verdict.

'Well,' said the young male doctor. 'How are we feeling today?' Well, I was actually feeling much better. I'd had a good night's sleep in a clean and comfortable place and I didn't have to struggle to work this day. I'd also been eating regular square hospital meals which included meat dishes that gave me the iron I was probably lacking. The nurses were so nice to me, like they really cared. I wouldn't have minded staying there forever. Obviously I was worried about what was happening to me but otherwise I was quite comfortable.

'Well,' the doctor continued, 'you young-ones' he paused for effect. That's when I noticed a team of other doctors and nurses were taking it in turns to look at my file and then one by one, they were smiling at me. 'The scan shows that you are carrying twins! - all is fine at the moment but obviously with this bleeding we need to keep a close eye on you, we'll keep you in for bed-rest for the time being and see how we get on.'

'Twins!' I said as my jaw hit the floor. And with that the team went on to their next patient who was told that she had miscarried and that she could go home.

I called Mark at his mum's and he was totally shocked, we both were but we felt blessed too. Maybe this was something that was just meant to be. Some kind of compensation to make up for all my sad years, a complete family in one go.

I was thrilled when the hospital staff kept me in, on bed-rest, for a further two weeks. I loved the feeling of being safe, protected, cared for and comfortable. Patients aren't meant to like hospital food but I loved it. Maybe my body was just so deprived of nutritious food, with vitamins and minerals, that I lapped it up. I honestly swear I would have stayed there forever it I could have.

Vicky heard that I'd been admitted to hospital and one day she came to visit me and she had my post with her - a letter from the finance company that'd been sent to the Stratford house. It read like this;

'Dear Jennifer, as you will be leaving soon to have your baby, we enclose your last pay cheque. Best

Wishes. Management.'

'Bastards!' Vicky shouted.

It was wrong and unacceptable, even in those days, to get rid of someone because they were pregnant. But as I'd been so useless, I really couldn't blame them for terminating my employment. Anyway, I actually felt relieved that I didn't have to make that arduous journey into central London anymore.

I was feeling much better and the nurses told me I could go home and to take it easy. I'd settled into the hospital routine and honestly would have preferred to have stayed. The thought of being back in Mark's squat-flat made me shudder. Although at the same time I missed him.

I was just sitting up in bed, waiting for my discharge papers as a middled-aged, blonde-haired woman suddenly showed up at my side. 'Hello, my name's Sally, I'm the Hospital Social Worker, I've been told you're being discharged today so, just wanted to check you're ok and happy with everything at home.'

Damn, I must have said something to one of the nurses, that'd alerted their attention and now the Social Services were sticking their noses into my life. Me and my big mouth! I had a natural distrust of social-workers from my experiences with the one called Derek, back in Worcester. He'd been, in the main, unhelpful, unkind and bordering on useless. He'd just ticked boxes to cover his own arse and picked up his pay cheque each month. But this Sally did have a kind face and she seemed different.

'Erm, well it's not a great situation, it's not really our flat you see and anyway there's no shower or bath and it's a bit of a dump' I explained. I didn't have much hope of any help from social workers but perhaps she had the power to keep me in the hospital! I had to give this one a chance. I decided to confide in her and to tell her everything.

'What about family, your support network? Your mum your dad?' She asked with genuine interest.

I proceeded to explain the whole sorry story; I hoped she had all day to listen.

'Well, this won't do at all! So, what practical steps can we take today?' She exclaimed, as I shrugged my shoulders in reply. 'Look, I'll sort out your social security benefits and then I'll get straight onto the council, get you onto their priority housing list at least.' Her voice sounded animated as she continued putting her pen to her note pad and writing down all of my details.

'But I can't prove addresses, I haven't lived around here for long enough' I proclaimed.

'Well, I think they can make an exception in your case' She insisted, as she gave my hand a reassuring squeeze.

She gave me a card with her telephone number on it, 'If you ever need anything, give me a call'

I'd heard that before, that was the exact same line that that Hospital Social Worker, in Worcester, had said to me and my sister. Derek was his name. He was the one who broke the news to us that our mother had just died. He turned out to be not much help at all. So, although this 'Sally' had made me feel hopeful, deep down I didn't expect any help from her either.

CHAPTER 16

Happy Birthday!

I was nearly four months pregnant and the size of a house already. I spent my days alone while Mark was out at work. When it got to around six pm I started to expect him back. But invariably he would go straight from work to his Mother's house for a shower or a bubble bath. Then he would have his dinner there and after that he'd generally go straight to the pub. I often wouldn't see him again until he came home in the evening at gone eleven pm. I was used to the smell of alcohol on his breath.

The days passed slowly like that. I'd watch the little ticker on the alarm clock going round and round for hours. Sometimes I'd watch television and if it cut I'd go to the shop and buy a packet of cheesy Wotsits to get some change. I needed fifty-pence pieces to start the television up again.

I needed a shower but there wasn't one so I would

boil up some pans in the kitchen and bring the plastic washing-up bowl into the living room to try to strip-wash. This is how you strip-wash with just one washing up bowl. Hands and face first then hair (that's the difficult bit) then, with the murky, soapy water and lastly - private parts. Then carry the warm water back and throw it down the kitchen sink. The real difficulty was the washing my hair section - trying to bend over double to a bowl on the floor, with a massive hard belly in the way, was really tough.

The evenings seemed even longer than the days. The loneliness was the worst thing and the only visitors I had were the mice. Sometimes I'd put a couple of cheesy-Wotsits down on the dirty lino, next to the record player, to deliberately encourage the mice in. I'd wait quietly in the dark for them. After a few minutes, one or two mice would come in and take their time nibbling away. It was entertaining to watch and some kind of company at least.

I didn't know any of the neighbours, I assumed everyone was renting. It was a transient area so renters came and went and people didn't bother to get to know one another much. I'd seen two young dark-skinned guys, one time, as they went in upstairs but I'd never spoken to them. We kept ourselves to ourselves. It was a rough area and the less people knew about you the safer you felt.

On occasion I went back to visit Vicky, Den and the

others. But the guys were scared of Mark and were afraid of getting on the wrong side of him. They'd seen him fighting several times and didn't want to anger him by having me over too often. They were worried he might suggest something was going on between one of them and me. So, I passed most days alone, at the squat-flat, waiting for my confinement.

One Sunday morning as Mark was getting ready to go out. 'Mark, Mark, Mark why you not answering?' I spoke.

'The way you say Mark really gets on my nerves' Marrk, Marrk!' He taunted.

I went quiet and thought for a moment. 'Look I'm really unhappy, I'm pregnant and'

'Yeah, you never stop going on about it' he interrupted.

'I don't wanna be left here all the time by myself!' I started to get choked up.

'Well ask me if I care?' he said, 'anyway I'm going to football.'

I sat on the corner of the bed watching Mark putting his Sunday league football kit into a sports bag. I knew he'd be gone for the day. On Sundays he normally played football in the morning. After the match, his whole team would go to the local pub for a few beers. Then he would go to his mums for Sunday roast dinner and after that he'd probably have a siesta on his mum's settee, have a shower and then go out to the Eddie. As he left, I played one of his records by his favourite band, ironically named The Cure.

'Yesterday I got so old, I felt like I could die'

'Yesterday I got so old, it made me want to cry'

'Go on, go on, just walk away, go on, go on your choice is made,'

'Go on, go on, and disappear, go on, go on away from here'

I couldn't bear my life. In reduced circumstances you have to believe in all kinds of things to get you through. I used to close my eyes and see myself playing out with my best-friend Lisa when we were children. We'd be laughing and joking as we climbed the Malvern hills on a sunny day.

I dreamed about owning a pair of pink fluffy slippers, like ballet shoes with satin ribbons. I regularly fantasised about them and about how the soft pink fluff would cover my feet like candy floss. One day I would be in a better place and I would own those slippers.

Time passed like that and by the end of September my twenty-first birthday came along. Normally your twenty-first birthday is a real milestone day. You really come of age on your twenty-first. It should be a wonderful occasion and a real celebration.

Vicky had gone to the trouble of arranging a little birthday party for me, back at the Stratford house. Of course, Mark and I were both invited although the guys (living at the Stratford house) were clearly going to be nervous about him being in their territory.

As Vicky was still living in the living room, the gathering had been set up in another part of the house. It was like a big corridor in the middle of the house, that always lacked natural daylight. The dark navy-blue carpets and grubby undecorated walls added to the grim interior. You might get the impression that these guys were poor. But in fact, they all had plenty of money. Den already owned the house outright. He'd paid off the mortgage early by constantly renting rooms and he'd saved money by never ever refurbishing any of the house except for his own bedroom. He was only in his thirties yet he was already able to retire. He spent his free-time riding around London on his motorbike or failing that, you'd find him propping up the bar in the Eddie. But I've digressed.

There were two second hand settees and a few wooden chairs that had been strategically placed for us visitors. Den and the guys were already sitting there, drinking lager. As I waddled in, one of them called out 'Happy Birthday!' and I said 'thanks' and by boyfriend followed me in. Then I sensed their nervousness and a change in the atmosphere. A respectful deportment towards Mark.

They were overly-polite, over-friendly. But their anxiousness would ease as the beers sank.

There was a little wobbly table leaning up against the wall with some food items on it. It seemed that Vicky had gone to the trouble of baking cup-cakes! As I went to help myself, she warned me that they were weed-cakes. Or maybe she described them as marijuana muffins. Even at the time I thought it was highly inappropriate to put drugs inside cup-cakes for a pregnant woman's birthday and I said so. 'Well, this couple over ere don't have any weed in em.' Vicky announced.

Well, I wasn't about to risk it, knowing my luck Vicky would have got them muddled up. No, I wouldn't risk that and anyway I was already too annoyed to eat anything. But at the same time, my feelings were mixed, as Vicky had been thoughtful to arrange the party for me. Of course, I didn't eat any of the cakes. Although Vicky insisted that 'just one bite' wouldn't harm the babies even if I did bite into the wrong muffin. But I stuck to my guns easily because I was so annoyed about it all. Yet at the same time, it was difficult to be angry with her when she'd gone to the trouble of arranging a birthday party for me.

Looking back, I suppose the cannabis cup-cakes showed Vicky's immaturity. The immaturity of all of them. I felt disappointed with the 'birthday party' as I sat watching Mark and the others tucking into my 'birthday weed-cakes.' They all started giggling soon after their consumption. I just stopped wanting to be there and I suppose I got into a bad mood. Mark picked up on it and started picking on me. Then I left unceremoniously. While the rest of them, including Mark, continued their evening at the Eddie. I took the bus back to the Manor Park flat. I lay, in almost darkness, watching the colony of mice coming and going by the light of the moon. The little alarm clock ticked. Tick-tock, tick-tock. Mark was blind drunk when he came home that night. And I pretended to be asleep.

A few days later I received a letter in the post, from Sally. She informed me that I was now on the housing waiting list and she was using her power of influence to elevate my position. That's something at least, I thought. When Mark and I have a proper place to live he'll not go round to his mums so much. He'll stop going to the pub all the time. He'll be happy to stay home with me and our little family.

It was October and I wasn't due until the end of February but I suddenly had terrible pain in my back. After doing all I could do to alleviate the pain, I struggled to the phone box, under the flyover. I called a taxi to take me to hospital. There I was checked over by an obstetrician who confirmed that all was well with the pregnancy. There were no signs of early labour. I hoped to be admitted to the prenatal ward but they said all was well and I could go back home.

'What's causing this terrible pain then?' I demanded.

'Well - I guess it's just that you're so tiny and having a first pregnancy with twins, you are growing so quickly so that's causing the pain', The doctor sounded like he knew what he was talking about. I made my way back home where I rolled around in pain for several hours more and then it seemed to pass. Maybe that doctor was right I concluded. (The doctor was right in so far as the pregnancy was concerned but the hospital never checked for anything else. A few years later, in a non-pregnant state, I was to again experience this terrible pain only to discover that I was suffering from kidney stones)

From then on the pains kept coming and going. Some days I was incapacitated with pain. One time Mark took me to the hospital and insisted I see a specialist right away. I was checked over and again convinced that all was well. The babies were fine and I was to stop worrying.

'I'm not worrying, I'm in agony' I cried.

My notes where checked and I was again sent home.

CHAPTER 17

Bed And Breakfast

A few days later I received another letter from Sally but this time the envelope included a map of part of Ilford and a request that I call her as soon as possible. So, I immediately made my way to the telephone box, under the flyover. Sally told me that I was now on the 'Priority Waiting list' for a council flat. Which meant that I was now officially under the council's care. My living conditions, at Mark's flat, had ticked all the boxes for 'highly inappropriate' and 'unsanitary conditions' And, that meant that arrangements had been made for me to check-in to a local hotel where I was to become a temporary resident, until my own flat became available. Sally was really proving to be a good social worker.

Mark seemed pleased that we'd be getting a council flat soon and didn't seem to mind me going to stay at the hotel. So, I packed up my bags and took a short bus ride into Ilford, armed with the map of Ilford and Sally's instructions. It took a while for me to locate the hotel. From the outside it just looked like a normal, big terrace house. Only it had a swinging sign reading 'Bed and Breakfast.'

I made my way into the reception area where an Indian man was obviously expecting me. Then with my room-key in hand, I passed through the living area where three men stopped talking, in their own language, and turned to stare at me. I continued onwards and upwards to the attic of the building before I located my room. I could hear men's voices speaking in foreign tongue of perhaps Arabic or Urdu. I had no idea but I started to rush to get into my room. I don't know why I felt so nervous and threatened by this environment, but I did.

In a rush to get into the sanctuary of my new room I urgently turned the key in the bedroom door. As I entered, I immediately felt a crushing disappointment. There was a small single bed with a brown bedspread, brown painted walls and a brown carpet of a slightly different shade. There were no windows except for a roof skylight. There was, what looked like, a cupboard door under the eaves, held ajar and I could see a toilet. A notice on the wall read that the shared showers could be located on the next floor down.

I dropped my bags and sat on the weak and wiry mattress of the bed. I could hear the men's voices echoing from the other rooms of the building. And

I said out loud, 'I can't sleep here,' I didn't want to appear rude or ungrateful as I made my way back down to the receptionist.

'Excuse me, is it possible to give me a different room please?' I pleaded.

'No that your room, no other room' The reception man replied.

'Ok thank you,' I said, as I placed the room-key on the counter-top and left the building.

I made my way back to Mark's flat.

The next day I took a bus to the council building in Stratford. I was worried when I told the lady that I'd been too scared to stay in the grim attic room, in a house full of foreign men. I thought that she might think I was racist or ungrateful for refusing this free accommodation. But actually, she was very nice and really understanding. She immediately made arrangements for me to check into a different hotel in an area just outside of Ilford, called Goodmayes.

The area of Goodmayes, used to be famous for its huge mental hospital and you'd often see people who looked like escapees, wondering around the area. Although it was difficult to know who was who. Mental ill health seemed to cross through the general public and I was no stranger to it myself. Still, I better hold on to my sanity or I'd be in danger of having my babies taken from me. So, later that afternoon, I prepared my bags and took two short bus journeys to Goodmayes'.

The Bed and Breakfast hotel was a little larger, from the outside, than the Ilford one. A pleasant English woman greeted me at Reception and gave me my room key. My room was on the ground floor, right next to the communal living area. The room was small but clean and tidy with flowery decor. The single bed was flush against the wall and there was a window which overlooked a flowered back garden. Most importantly, I had my own en suite toilet and shower! Pure luxury.

I wandered into the living room, to have a look around, and there I met another few of the residents. There were two other pregnant English girls of a similar age to myself. One had her boyfriend staying with her and they apparently had a double room. The other girl was single. They were both in their nightdresses. Apparently, they didn't bother dressing for breakfast either. This seemed such a nice and relaxed atmosphere.

I took a shower and had an early night. I slept so well on a comfortable bed and next morning, still wearing my pyjamas, I went to the breakfast area. The husband of the receptionist-lady was serving and he seemed very nice and polite. He was a grey-ing, middle-aged man who the others called Don. He seemed to have a glint in his eye for me and I guessed he was just the flirty type. He asked my preferred name then continued to make jolly conversation with me and the other residents. Everyone was laughing at Don's droll banter and I raised a smile too.

Most days I had nothing much to do so I'd take the two busses back to Mark's flat. I still had my own door key to come and go as I pleased. The place was getting colder as winter was approaching. There was an emptiness and an echo as my shoe landed on the hard lino of the entrance hall. It didn't compare to the warm atmosphere of the hotel. Mark wasn't always there and sometimes when he was, he often seemed off. I was pleasantly surprised on the occasions when he seemed more pleased to see me. Anyway, I was glad Sally had made arrangements to get me into Bed and Breakfast. Even though the first hotel hadn't worked out, the second one was great.

One Sunday afternoon I went to visit Mark. But as I arrived at the flat, he was about to leave. He'd been to Sunday league football but he'd forgotten his cash. So, he'd only popped back to pick up his wallet and then wouldn't be back again for several hours. So, I sat alone for half an hour. I didn't see the mice as they tended not to appear during the daylight hours. I sat there thinking and watching the little hand tik-tok on Mark's alarm clock. Then I got up and made my way back to the Goodmayes hotel.

When I got to the hotel, I was really tired and so, for comfort, I changed into a nightdress. No one was about so I went and put the television on in the living room. I relaxed on one of the communal settees and then I lay down.

Then I heard the chatting of two male voices. I recognised Don's voice but didn't know the other. Then the two stumbled into the living room. I didn't bother to sit up as it was normally such a relaxed environment and we were encouraged to treat it like our home. Don was clearly inebriated and they'd obviously both just returned from the local public house. Don's face lit up when he saw me laying there. My huge bump now raised up like the Worcestershire beacon. His friend smiled and appeared slightly less intoxicated as he followed Don over towards me. Don was smiling and talking and getting closer and closer. Then with his arms outstretched he slurred, 'Can I feel the baby kick?' Well, I'd never liked anyone touching my pregnant bump, not even Mark. I hardly even touched it myself. But I felt rude to say no. So, I sort of smiled and said nothing as his hands landed on my belly. I gave a slightly embarrassed look towards the other guy who was smiling that obligatory smile that people give to pregnant women.

Don rubbed his hands up and down on my left and rights sides. Then his hands suddenly drove up and strongly cupped my breasts! I knocked them away with a reflex movement. I looked at the other guy, who's smile had suddenly dropped, perhaps in shock (hopefully horror and disgust) at his friend's behaviour.

I struggled to sit up, then stood up, then quickly walked out to meet the sanctuary of my bedroom. I closed the door abruptly. I was now safe. No, I wasn't safe! Of course, Don had the keys to all of the rooms in the house including mine. Was he locating them now? What was he planning? And what was the other guy thinking!?

I grabbed a bag and threw my clothes into it. I grabbed another bag and everything else went in there. Tooth brush, hair brush, a magazine that I'd borrowed from the living room. I couldn't even bend to check under the bed. Within two minutes I vacated the room and left the room-key in the door. I shot out of the hotel wearing a nightdress with socks and shoes and a jacket on top. I left as quickly as my legs would allow.

When Mark sobered up, I told him what had happened. He became really angry. 'Me an me brothers a gonna smash ees head open wiv a baseball bat. Ees dead meat I tell ya'

I couldn't help thinking that Mark was more concerned about Don disrespecting him than any concern he might have had for the assault on me. I regretted telling Mark as he just made me nervous by saying how he was going to beat up Don. I believed him. He never asked what I wanted. But in the end, I think it was all bravado anyway. In the end he did nothing about it.

CHAPTER 18

New Life

I was afraid to let the council know that I'd left the second Bed and Breakfast hotel. I thought they might think I was lying about what Don had done. I was worried that by walking out I'd now jeopardised my chances of getting a council flat. But the council-lady was really nice about it. I was concerned about other vulnerable girls being placed at the Goodmayes hotel in the future. And she assured me that no other single girls would be sent there. It never crossed my mind to go to the police and she never suggested it. What Don had done was unprovable and I didn't want to upset his wife by bringing the episode to her attention. Anyway, I suppose no physical harm was done.

I was back living in Mark's cold squat-flat and on the last Thursday in November, I received a letter from the council. I'd been offered a council flat in Forest gate which was exactly half-way in between

Ilford and Stratford. It was the best news ever! Sally had turned out to be highly conscientious and caring. I vowed never to say bad things about Social Workers ever again.

Mark took the Friday off work and together we got the keys from the council and went to look at our new place. It was a two bedroom ground floor flat in a quiet street in a reasonably good area. The decorative order was good and I loved it. Finally I had a home, a stable and permanent home!

I accepted the tenancy on the flat right away but we would need a few more nights at Mark's place before we could properly move in. There was paperwork to do and the amenities needed to be switched on. I was claiming benefits and Sally had arranged for a lump sum to be paid out from them so that we could get a second-hand cooker and a bed. I felt like Christmas had come early this year.

On the Saturday lunchtime I met up with Vicky at the Eddie. It was the last day of November. I wasn't drinking or smoking anymore but a chat and an orange juice would do me the world of good. As usual, Linda and Annie were there too. Linda was friendly and even Annie managed a smile after staring at my bump for a moment. Pregnant women had a weird trance effect on some people.

Vicky and I left the pub to go and look around the second-hand furniture shops. It was surprisingly cold and on our way I watched a sprinkle of snow as it landed on the belly of my jumper dress. I could no longer close my jacket as my bump protruded out so much and my belly felt cold. As the snowflake floated down, I went into a kind of trace state for a minute and then everything seemed to go into slow motion for a few seconds and I had a whooshing sound in my ears. As I came out of it, Vicky was looking at me with a confused or concerned expression.

'You ok?' Vicky questioned.

I managed a half smile and shrugged my shoulders. 'It's snowing Vic, don't ya think snow is similar to candy floss?' I said.

'What the ell are you on about?' She continued to stare at me with a frown.

'I want some pink slippers' I continued.

'Think you've had too much orange juice' Vicky smiled.

It was lovely to spend time with Vicky as we hardly saw each other lately. She explained that she intended to leave Den's house soon. She was in the process of making arrangements to go back to live in south London. She said it was where she belonged. We strolled around and chatted and enjoyed our time together. Then the pain hit me and I went quiet.

'You ok Jen?' Vicky enquired.

'Yeah, it's just this terrible pain I've been having on

and off for weeks, it's ok I've seen the doctors and they say it's nothing' I struggled to speak.

'It don't look like nothing Jen' Vicky's voice showed concern, 'I could see it on your face just then, that's terrible pain you're in, I could see it!'

'Yeah, it's bad Vick, really bad, but what can I do, they say the twins are ok, they say it's just cause I'm small.' I wanted to cry but I held back the tears. 'Anyway, the pains are passing quicker now, last month it was constant and now it's just coming and going. See I'm alright now, see it's passed again.'

After that, Vicky said that I didn't quite seem myself and I should get the bus back to the flat. So, we said our goodbyes.

Back at the flat and Mark was getting ready for his Saturday night out. He was concerned about my suffering but not concerned enough to stop him going out and enjoying the evening. Anyway, by now he was used to seeing me in pain and anguish. He was convinced, by the professionals, that all was ok.

He gave me a hug, 'See ya later' he said.

There was usually a student party on, on a Saturday night, after the pub closed, but I hoped Mark would at least forfeit that and come home at eleven. Surely he would. For he knew I was suffering. The pains kept coming and going, coming and going. I rolled around in agony. 'I'm going to have to call the hospital.' I thought to myself. 'If I don't get to the phone box soon, I'm going to struggle to get there at all,' I thought. So, I made my way slowly and tentatively to the flyover telephone box.

'Hello Maternity' a young female voice answered.

'Hello I'm twenty-eight weeks pregnant with twins, I'm in terrible pain, the pain keeps coming and going, I don't know what to do?' I was frantic and it showed in my voice.

The nurse took my name and other details and disappeared for a few minutes. I assumed she was checking my notes. I suppose my notes read that I'd been in several times already with pain. The pregnancy was normal and that I was an overanxious first-time mum.

'Aww is it your first baby?'

'Yes, but its twins' I replied.

'Alright now what you do is, you have lots of nice warm drinks and just relax and just stay next to the phone and call us again if you feel any worse ok - you're not by yourself are you?'

'Yes, I am, my boyfriend's gone to the pub and I don't have a home-phone, I'm at the phone box, under the Ilford flyover'

'Alright so what you do is, just go back home and stay nice and warm ok?'

'Ok, so I shouldn't come in then?' I questioned.

'No, you just go home at relax,' she repeated.

'Oh ok, thank you, bye'

What could I do? They were the professionals, they should know best. I waddled down to the sweet shop and bought a packet of cheesy Wotsits, (to share with the mice) a bar of chocolate and a fizzy orange drink. By the time I got back to the flat I was in excruciating pain. I couldn't eat the chocolate so I just threw it on the bed, I managed a couple of sips of the fizzy orange. Then I ripped the cheesy Wotsits bag open and emptied the whole packet on the floor, for the mice.

It was around 10pm and I prayed Mark would not go on to a party tonight. That he would consider my condition on this night. But I guess after a couple of beers, Mark didn't think about me much.

By midnight I sat on the toilet and had an urge to push down. I had no idea why. I had no idea what was happening. The babies weren't due until the first of March, which was an odd coincidence as that was my dead mum's birthday. I struggled back to the back bedroom and lay on the bed.

'Help me!!' I cried out, but no one came.

I crawled on hands and knees to the empty, damp living room at the front of the house. I don't know why I went there. I lay on the filthy red carpet, in the dark, and rolled around. After a few more minutes I went to the toilet again and pushed down. Then I noticed a little pink patch on my underwear. I didn't know what it was and I was passed caring. I noticed the mice making their way into the bedroom, as I passed through, on my way back to the living room. I lay on the floor again in a state of delirious pain and panic. I moaned and groaned for hours.

'Help Me!!!' I called, but even if I'd have been a choir of fifty women, no one would have heard me over the main road traffic. And even if someone had heard, I doubt anyone would have come.

At 4am I heard Mark's key in the door. 'I'm in here Mark, please help me' I called out from the living room floor.

'Watcha doing in ere babe?' Mark lay down beside me his breath reeking of alcohol.

'Help me! I'm in terrible pain, please get me to the hospital, please call an ambulance!' I begged.

'Alright easy' Mark slurred. 'I'll get you a taxi' He stood up and stumbled out of the flat.

Around twenty minutes later and I could hear two voices on the doorstep. Mark and what I guessed was the taxi driver. Next thing Mark was trying to stand me up and he managed to lift me to my feet and push me into the rear of the waiting car while the Nigerian driver looked on in horror. Mark bent my legs in and then closed the back door of the car.

'You'll be alright babe, they'll probably just send you back home, I'll see ya in the morning alright' He could hardly stand so he wobbled back into the ground floor and closed the front door.

'He don't come with you?' the driver asked.

'No please, please just get me to Newham general hospital'

I had three strong pains in the back of the taxi on a ten-minute journey. The driver sped to the hospital. The streets were almost empty as it was the early hours of Sunday morning. It was the first day of December.

On arrival, the driver shot out of the car and came running back with a hospital porter. They dragged me out of the car together. Next I was on a trolley and someone was looking up between my legs with a light. 'Jennifer, we are going to deliver you, ok?' A female voice said. This might be hard to believe but this was the point when I realised, I was in labour.

Suddenly the sleepy hospital went onto red alert. The porter was pushing my trolley fast and a nurse was running along the side of me. Double doors flung open into a dark theatre and then suddenly all the lights flickered on. Next a whole team came running in, looking sleepy eyed but they soon shot into action.

'Why on earth did you leave it so late to come into

hospital? How long have you been having contractions? 'If you'd have come in earlier, we could have prevented this premature labour with a drip' 'Why didn't you call us!' Voices came from all directions.

'Please help me! Please!' I pleaded.

'I'm the midwife Jennifer and I'm going to deliver you now, I'm afraid there's no time for analgesics but try to calm down now and take some deep breaths like you've learned in your antenatal classes' She spoke with a calm voice that was obviously disguising her total panic.

'My classes haven't started yet; they're meant to start next week!' I managed to reply before the next powerful contraction.

Twenty-five minutes after I arrived at the hospital, my baby boy arrived. He was the tiniest human I'd ever seen. I was stunned and shocked by his size. He weighed less than two pounds. (Less than a kilogram) I could see his tiny lungs were working hard as a nurse showed him to me for a few seconds and then raced him off to the special care baby unit. Then half an hour later and an awkward breach-birth ensued. My tiny girl was bruised from the difficult breach entry into the world. She struggled to breath as she followed her brother into intensive care.

I lay in shock in a pool of warm liquids. I assumed it was a combination of amniotic fluid, blood and hospital products. The theatre emptied out and I was left alone. Due to my muscle's physical exhaustion and the trauma of the last 24 hours, I was literally unable to move. I tried to reach the nurse's call buzzer but failed. They'd left it just out of reach. I was no longer the priority. There were two gravely ill new-borns to deal with. Eventually two new faces came in to clean me up and they called a porter who took me to the post-natal ward. Then a little time later -

'Would you like us to call anyone for you?' A kindly nurse was leaning over me as I lay in a freshly made bed.

"What time is it?" I was feeling disorientated.

It was Sunday afternoon at around 4.15pm. Almost twelve hours had passed since I'd arrived in the hospital.

From my bed I could hear the nurses, at their desk, in the corridor. The telephone rang and one of them answered the call. 'Yes, yes and you are? Ok yes, I see, well she's had them, a boy and a girl, - SCBU, erm Special Care Baby Unit, erm intensive care, yes, she's ok, yes visiting is normally three until five but we can make an exception for you, ok bye.'

Mark had woken up with a hangover and gone to Sunday league football as usual. Then he'd gone to his mum's house for Sunday roast and a nice hot shower. It was late afternoon by the time he'd realised I was still at the hospital and he'd discovered he was now a father. He then urgently made his way to the hospital.

'I'm so sorry babe, I didn't know you was in labour, I thought it was just the usual pains,' He was genuinely sorry.

In shock at what had happened, I felt myself going in and out of reality. I had to pinch myself to believe it all. Nothing made sense. Was I now a mum? I guess I was traumatised and Mark's familiar face was my only comfort. I felt no anger towards him. That's strange to me now.

That evening two ambulances transferred the twins and myself to another hospital. The unit at Newham general hospital hadn't been open long and was unable to cope with two very premature babies on top of their other patients. So one ambulance transferred the twins and I followed in a second ambulance.

'There's not enough space for two incubators and the four nurses and you as well,' said a sweet nurse. 'But I'll accompany you in the second ambulance. We're going to Wittington Hospital in North London where there's a well-established SCBU. There'll have the best of chances there.'

She was right. They did have the best of chances there. The doctors and nurses worked tirelessly, around the clock, caring for all the new-borns in the unit. In the first week, my two were doing well all things considered, it was I that needed to go into theatre to have the remainder of the placenta removed. One of the two had been accidentally left inside and was now infected. I was now dangerously anaemic, I lost too much blood and a transfusion was imperative. By the second week I was a little stronger but the roller coaster ride of having two sick babies was exhausting.

'It's their lungs you see, underdeveloped at that gestation' One of the paediatricians explained.

The staff always kept me involved with their care as much as possible. I learned all about their tubes and drips and lung drains and brain taps. I was like an expert the nurses joked.

While I was in hospital, Vicky sorted out the second-hand cooker and a mattress, with the payment from the social. She then moved back to live in south east London or her 'neck of the woods' as she called it.

The gas and electricity were both now connected in the council flat. And Mark had moved all of our personal belongings into what would now be our new home.

CHAPTER 19

Infidelity

After two weeks, I was well enough to go home but the babies would obviously not be able to leave for a while. The hospital had made arrangements and footed the bill to get me home in a taxi, seeing as they'd moved me from Newham General in the first place. Sally contacted me at the hospital, just before I left, and said she'd meet me at the council flat soon after I arrived. Mark was already at the flat waiting for me but he disappeared when he discovered Sally was on her way.

It was late afternoon and already dark when Sally arrived. 'I'll put the kettle on and we'll have a nice cup of tea and a chat about everything shall we?' Sally began.

'Well, we don't have any tea and there's no kettle' I replied.

'You mean you've come out of hospital after giving birth to twins and having a blood transfusion and he hasn't even got you anything to eat or drink?' Sally said with a despairing tone.

I just shook my head and forced a half smile.

'Look I'm going to pop out and I'll be back again in half an hour, an hour tops, ok?' I detected a little irritation in Sally's usually sweat demeanour. 'Just relax on the bed and I'll be as quick as I can.' I lay down on the mattress and let Sally pull the quilt up and over my legs.

Around forty five minutes later came a knock on the door and Sally entered with two carrier bags full of stuff. She'd been to the supermarket and bought, tea bags, milk, biscuits, bread and butter and she'd been to her office at the hospital and taken the kettle.

'I can't believe Mark didn't bother to get you anything' She started, 'to be honest I'm really upset with him, what's wrong with him?' She continued.

'I don't know Sally, but thank you so much for everything' I said.

'Look I'm going to order you a pizza delivery' Sally went on.

'No, I can't accept that' I replied.

'It's alright I'll put it on expenses, I'm hungry so I'll stay and eat with you' she insisted.

'Ok thanks' I said.

Sally was one of a kind - an angel. I'd despised social workers for a while and more specifically 'hospital social workers' The one I'd been assigned to in Worcester, at the age of fifteen, had been useless. More than that, he'd deliberately turned his back on me and closed the case. I suppose his paperwork covered him and his boss never knew. Sally was different; she'd renewed my faith in social workers.

It was around 8pm when Sally left and Mark turned up soon afterwards.

'I've got something to tell ya,' he began.

'What is it?' I replied nervously.

I knew something was up and I was dreading what Mark was about to tell me. He looked a bit fidgety as he sat down and put his arm around me. 'I've been with someone else' he announced.

'What?' I spoke.

'I slept with another bird, I'm sorry babe.' He continued.

This was just too much; after all I'd been through. How could he do that to me?

'Who is she?' I suddenly felt anger rising.

I needed to know who'd gone with him behind my back. I instinctively knew it was likely to be a girl from the pub. But who would be so disloyal to me as to go with my man while I was away in hospital and at my lowest ebb. I braced myself for his reply.

'I ain't gonna tell ya Jen' he said.

'You ain't gonna tell me! You left me alone to give birth by myself and now this!?' I felt like I was going to explode.

'Oh, here we go, I knew you was gonna start bringing that up sooner or later' he smirked.

'Get out, just get out!' I screamed.

He grabbed his leather jacket and the door slammed behind him.

I cried and cried, firstly with anger then with sadness and then with fear. I felt scared and lonely in the flat and couldn't face spending the night alone. On top of that, the responsibility of having two infants in intensive care was just too much to cope with by myself. And the more I thought about Mark going with another girl the more I realised I'd just thrown him into her arms by telling him to get out! History had repeated itself as my mother had done the exact same thing.

It was a twenty-minute walk to the Eddie at a fast pace, if I cut through the back streets. I felt sure Mark would be there and she (whoever she was) would be there too. I had to find out who she was, so I walked there in an energetic frenzy.

The pub was packed with loads of animated faces congratulating me on the birth of the twins but I could barely raise a smile. A collection had been made in one of those half-pint glasses. There was a sticker on the glass that read 'Collection for Mark's babies' Someone thrust the glass into my hands.

I held onto the half-pint glass that was heavy with coins and green pound-notes. I scanned the joint with my desperate eyes. Who is she and where is she?

Linda was making her way over in my direction and I expected her usual friendly approach but as she spotted me, she lowered her head and avoided eye contact. She was acting like she hadn't seen me but I knew she had. I was devastated as I instantly realised it must be her! How could she do that? She had always been so nice and so friendly. Now while everyone else was congratulating me, she had suddenly avoided me altogether. Pretending not to see me. She was obviously guilty. I had my answer.

Then I found Mark and we immediately left the pub together. We walked in the dark, cold night in silence with only the stream from our breath giving the appearance of conversation. As we arrived at the flat, I started.

'I know who it is' I began.

'No ya don't' he replied.

'Yes, I do' my voice started breaking.

'Who is it then?' Mark was slightly drunk and smirking.

'It's Linda' I said.

'What makes you think that?' he continued.

'I just knew it, I sensed it, it was obvious by the way she looked at me - well she avoided looking at me' I blurted out as my distress overwhelmed me.

'Well, you're wrong, cause it ain't Linda, it's Annie' he had a look of accomplishment on his face as though he'd won the game by me being unable to guess correctly.

'Annie!!' I screamed! 'She's supposed to be a Hospital Social Worker! She's supposed to be caring about people, what's wrong with her. What's wrong with people! She's not even attractive, she's so plane and dumpy. I just don't understand'

'Oh, she's really nice, a proper kind person, she might not be much to look at but she's got a nice personality' Mark stated.

'Oh my God what's wrong with you?' I was furious and devastated at the same time. I couldn't even piece my emotions together.

We'd been arguing for some time and we'd migrated to the hall next to the front door. I'm not sure who pushed who first but I remember slapping Mark around the face and him slapping me. And then a blow to the side of my head and multi-coloured stars appeared as my back slid down the wall that was directly behind me. As I was about to hit the floor, he put his hands underneath my armpits and yanked me back onto my feet, I felt drunk. I staggered away from him and into the bedroom where I landed on the mattress. I heard the front door slam shut. I cried and cried. The night passed with me going in and out of a restless sleep.

CHAPTER 20

Christmas

The following day I managed to get to the Whittington hospital to visit. Which was difficult as I was incapable of going on the underground train. I knew that if I did, I would become very unwell and no one would help me. I felt ill in every sense. I was physically weak and mentally even weaker. The busses seemed to take forever.

On arrival, at the hospital, I noticed all of the Christmas decorations were up in the Special Care Baby Unit. Then the nurses told me how the twins were doing. It was unlikely that they would survive their early birth unscathed. If they did survive, they were likely to be blind, deaf, mentally retarded or even in wheelchairs for life. The nurses were kind yet painfully honest with their details. But there was also a slim chance that they'd survive and thrive without ailments. I was still praying and betting on that.

There were six very sick babies in the unit, including my two who were parallel to each other. I sat on a stool in between the two incubators as the machine's beeped on a low volume and the radio played cheerful music.

'You better watch out'

'You better not cry'

'You better be sure'

'I'm telling you why'

'Santa Clause is coming to town'

'Santa Clause is coming to town'

'Santa Clause is coming to town'

I watched the angels working and caring for hours. One of the nurses mentioned that there was a parent-room right next-door to the baby unit and as it was unoccupied this night. I could stay over in there, which would save me travelling backwards and forwards on the busses.

Although I didn't have any overnight bag, I decided I would stay and I was shown to the parent-room. It was basic and the double bed swamped me. But I felt comfortable there especially as there was a machine with cheap little emergency tooth brushes and paste. Of course, I purchased a packet.

I could hear the vague and constant beeping of intensive care machinery all night. On occasion a louder more high-pitched siren would bleep. I instinctively knew those alarms were alerting the nurses of immediate danger. On occasion I would get up to check all was ok and the nurses would insist I go back to bed and get some rest. They re-assured me that everything was under control.

The next afternoon, I rode the buses back to the council flat. I felt very lonely until Mark turned up in the evening. I'm ashamed to admit it but I was pleased to see him. He was terribly sorry about fighting with me and promised not to meet up with Annie ever again. Although seeing her in the pub would be unavoidable. Frequenting a different pub - unthinkable.

On Christmas eve we were invited to stay over-night at Mark's mum's house, along with his two brothers and their girlfriends. One of them had just found out she was pregnant so it was all meant to be a combination of celebration.

That's one Christmas that I just cannot recall. It's strange I cannot recall it as I do have a photo-graph of it. I have a vague recollection of Mark's mum taking a photograph of we three couples. I guess Mark and I were first, him being the eldest of the three. The photograph was taken in his mum's posh room. She had two downstairs recep-tion rooms in her council house and no one was allowed into the posh one, unless it was Christmas. And as it was Christmas that's where the photo-graph was taken. His mum was very house proud and didn't have many visitors as they might mess it up. I suppose she made an exception at Christmas. Mark's dad wasn't there as his parents had been divorced a long while.

On Boxing Day, Mark and I made our way to the hospital. The babies had put weight on by now. They had grown so much but that's irrelevant really. It's irrelevant as it doesn't help anything.

'They've both had significant bleeds in the brain and we've done several brain-taps to drain off the excess fluid,' He was the specialist paediatrician and he spoke with a practiced mixture of tact and matter of fact. 'I have to tell you that it's likely that they will both end up possibly blind or possibly deaf or both, they might also be wheelchair bound.' My mind went numb and I couldn't comprehend what he'd just said. 'Are you ok? Do you understand what I've just explained to you?' 'Nurse, can you get mum a cup of tea'

There's nothing you can say to that, you just keep hoping that it's not true and your mind just can't take it in. You hear, all the time, about doctor's being wrong and making mistakes. You hear, all the time, about miraculous recoveries, don't you?

That was the first time I saw Mark cry. We'd got back to the flat and he'd gone into what should have been, the babies' room and picked up the pink and white stripy baby grow and the blue and white one. He sat on the floor and held one in his left hand and one in his right hand and he sobbed. I tried to comfort him but to no avail. He was just inconsolable.

Then he packed a small bag and said he was going to his mum's but I think he went to Annie. He left his records behind.

'Go on, go on, just walk away'

'Go on, go on, your choice is made'

'Go on, go on and disappear'

'Go on, go on away from here'

'And I know I was wrong, when I said it was true'

'That it couldn't be me, and be her in between,'

'Without you, without you'

CHAPTER 21

Scrubs

From time to time, I would go to the local telephone box in Forest Gate and call the hospital to check the situation.

'You need to come here straight away' the nurse insisted, 'he's not holding his own anymore.'

That was the expression the nurses used. What they meant was that the tiny boy was doing nothing by himself anymore. The machines were literally doing everything for him. 'It's kinder to let him go' they said on my arrival at the special care unit. 'With your consent, we will place him in your arms and switch off the life support, it's better for him like that, he'll know his mum's holding him and it's better for you too, otherwise we'll just call you one day and he'll be gone and that'll be much worse for you and him. We can do no more for him really, we are so sorry'

I called Mark's mum for her to let Mark know the

situation. Then after signing some forms, I was placed in a comfortable chair next to the incubator and my baby boy was placed in my arms for the first and last time. Most of the machines were disconnected leaving just the heart monitor which periodically set an alarm off as the heartbeats became weaker and weaker. A nurse turned the volume down to try and prevent it upsetting me and within a matter of twenty minutes, my baby boy was pronounced dead.

Then the kind nurse allowed the rules to be broken by allowing me to keep my boy in my arms. She covered him in a white blanket and wrapped my jacket around my shoulders. She grabbed some paperwork and we walked together, to the morgue, under the cover of darkness. There, he was prised out of my arms and I was forced to let him go.

The funeral was arranged and paid for by the hospital and two of the nurses kindly gave up their free time to attend. Mark and all of his family turned up to show their respects. Luckily, I had the nurses otherwise I'd have felt like I had no one to represent my side.

Afterwards, the nurses went off to work and Mark's family all came back to the council flat. It was the first time his mum had been. After a couple of hours, they all left accept Mark. We comforted each other and he stayed. The following day he moved his stuff back in.

The following week the nurses assured me that my girl was doing well. They said that sometimes all the strength goes from one twin to the other in this situation. They said his strength had almost certainly gone to his sister. She was putting weight on and was almost looking like the size of a healthy baby, born at full gestation.

A week or so after my baby boy's funeral, I went to do one of my interim telephone calls to the hospital. They were relieved that I'd called as they'd been trying to work out a way to contact me, they were actually going to send the police. Because my girl had suddenly taken a turn for the worse and I should come to the Special Care Baby Unit immediately.

As previously mentioned, there'd been a whip-round at the pub and I'd been given a half-pint glass full of coins and pound-notes. I was supposed to buy the babies some clothes with this money but I hadn't gotten round to it. And in the back of my mind, I wasn't sure they'd both make it. All in all, there was approximately twenty quid in there. But I'd already spent some of the coins on trips to the telephone box.

I went back to my flat and grabbed the half-pint glass full of coins. Then I ran around to the nearest taxi-rank. I asked the taxi driver to put his foot down and within half an hour I was at the hospital. I thrusted the whole glass of coins into the driver's hands as he looked at me in confusion. I heard his voice say, 'hey!' as I slammed the car door shut. I ran through the car park and through the hospital corridors. Left then straight then right then straight again. I knew the way. I was in a terrible fluster when I arrived.

A female nurse and a male doctor met me at the entrance to intensive care. They guided me through to a side room with comfortable chairs. We sat down and they looked at me, both anticipating the other would speak first. The doctor spoke, 'I'm so sorry to tell you, your baby-daughter died just before you arrived, about half an hour ago.' I just put my face in my hands and cried a river. The thought that she'd gone and that she'd died without me being there to hold her.

The incubator had already been switched off, except for the lights. All signs of supportive equipment had been removed and my daughter was already wrapped in her shroud. It was better to let the porter take her over to the morgue this time, they said. It was still daylight hours and no one wanted to see a bereft mum carrying a dead baby across the hospital grounds. I could always visit there before the funeral.

The nurses said that someone would contact me from a bereavement service and that I would be invited back to the unit sometimes, so that I didn't feel cut out from it all. They understood that after spending so much time visiting intensive care, parents could suddenly feel at a loss or rejected when a baby died and there was no longer any reason to continue visiting the unit. Parents then felt unwelcome. So, to make them feel welcome and to aid their emotional recovery, they would periodically be invited to visit, as part of the bereavement service. But I never heard from them again. I guess I slipped through their net.

All of Mark's family turned up on the day of the funeral but there was no one on my side. I guess the nurses were too busy or it was just too distressing for them to come. I really didn't blame them.

During the days and weeks that followed, Mark drank more and more. We were both unable to cope with our losses and we argued a lot. On occasion he hit me. The neighbours sometimes called the police because of my high-pitched screaming. The police usually took Mark away and kept him in a cell overnight. One officer was assigned to the case, and he discussed with me some options such as me going into a women's refuge. I really couldn't face that.

Sometimes I'd split up with Mark because of his aggressive behaviour towards me but I always took him back. I loved him, I missed him, I was lost and lonely without him and most importantly, I had no other family or friends. I felt the only way to ever replace what I'd lost was via him. Whenever he returned he was always so sorry and so pathetic that I felt sorry for him. I felt unbearable and misplaced guilt! When he told me everything would be ok I wanted to believe it.

One night I was sitting on the living room floor, watching television, while Mark was out at the pub. By this time, we had a second-hand settee that looked quite nice but wasn't very comfortable so I usually sat in front of it, on the floor. I'd started to feel nervous whenever I heard the key enter the front door. I was severely underweight and living on my nerves. I was one hundred percent living on empty. And by that, I mean, my womb was now empty of life, my stomach was empty of food. But also, in general, I was devoid of love. Emotionally, I was utterly empty. There was no reason to even live anymore, there was nothing but emptiness.

So, on this night, I heard footsteps and the jangling of keys, and my heart began to race, as it did lately, from anxiety. Mark's key took a while to turn in the front-door and then suddenly he tripped in and was standing in the doorframe of the living room. I looked up at him as he towered over. He looked particularly drunk and kind of vicious.

'Don't fucking start' The whites of his eyes were bloodshot-red and he was swaying back and forth aggressively. As if he were drunkenly psyching himself for battle.

'I didn't say anything' I attempted a half smile. His senses were hindered from excessive alcohol consumption but he could always smell my fear and it riled him.

'Don't fucking start!!' He said, as he staggered towards me.

'It's ok, I'm not starting, just sit down' I attempted to stand up with the intention of encouraging him to sit down on the settee. But God knows what he thought my intentions were, in his drunken stupor.

'Don't fucking start!!' He shouted, as his hands reached down to grab the scruff of my collar.

'No, please don't' I begged' As I tried to reason with the unreasonable.

To the sound of my pleading, he picked me up off the floor, by the scruff of my neck and slapped me around the face twice, left and then right. I managed to resist his grasp as I dropped back down to my sitting position on the floor, at the foot of the settee. He staggered back a few paces like a bull before an attack. Through his drunken muffled ears, the sound coming from the television seemed to attract his attention. Then with a run and a drop-kick he put his steel-toe-capped boot through the centre of the big old television screen and it banged with a shockingly loud, electrically powered explosion!

Then the room fell silent as millions of particles of fiberglass fluttered down like snowflakes. Everything went into slow-motion as my ears rang and I had a flashback of the snowflake landing on the pregnant belly of my jumper dress. Then I visualised my mother's grave covered in snow, when I was sixteen. It was my first winter without her and her gravestone hadn't gone up yet. I was panicking as I was searching, unable to locate it, unable to find her. Then further back in time and I was a happy young child throwing snowballs with my friends in Hollymount. Then there was more ringing in my ears as I must have gone into shock.

Mark's boots were not finished yet. He turned to look at me as I tried to quickly get myself onto the settee and up off of the floor. Then as though he were taking a penalty, in a Sunday league football match, he took a step back and then ran and kicked with all his might. His right boot made perfect contact with my right buttock. I travelled a meter across the living room and felt a searing pain that took my breath away. I crumpled up on the floor defenceless and finished. Black dots darkened the glare of the electric lighting.

I don't know if Mark had left the front door open but next thing I remember, the police were in the flat. The neighbours must have called them again. Mark was immediately arrested as he told the police to 'fuck off' as soon as he saw them.

'You alright love?' it was the same police officer that was assigned to my case. 'We better get you checked at the hospital'

That night Mark was kept in the police cells as I went off to Newham general hospital. He was then transferred to Wormwood Scrubs, a high security prison on the other side of London. They could only keep him in for a week and then they would charge him with 'actual bodily harm.' They would press the charges - not me. I suppose they kept him in Scrubs to give me a little breathing space. I had a suspected fractured pelvis, but an x-ray showed it was in fact only very bad bruising.

'Yesterday I got so scared, I shivered like a child'

'Yesterday away from you, it froze me deep inside'

'Come back, come back, don't walk away'

'Come back, come back, come back today'

'Come back, come back, why can't you see'

'Come back, come back, come back to me'

I know I shouldn't say this but while Mark was away, I missed him, and I learnt why abused women stay with their abusers. Don't expect me to have any self-respect here. Self-respect is something we learn in our teenage years. And if you don't learn it then it's almost impossible to learn it as an adult as you keep being drawn to those who disrespect you and it becomes perpetual. A self-fulfilling prophecy.

After my mother's death, my remaining family had taught me the language of disrespect and now I couldn't relate to respect, especially in love-relationships which meant - with males. My family had rejected me, disrespecting me most severely and all I now knew was how to be disrespected, how to disrespect myself and how to live with the disrespectful. How crazy is this, I even thought that the violence Mark showed towards me, proved how much he cared for me. Surely, he couldn't get so angry about someone he didn't care about! The energy he'd put into such aggression was somehow 'love' in my confused mind.

I hated being alone in the flat. I felt nothing but grief and fear. In fact, after all the years I'd spent desperately wanting a permanent home, now I had it - I felt no connection to it. No connection at all. I even considered leaving it and giving up the tenancy. But there was nowhere else to go. After a couple of days of unbearable loneliness, a massive black and blue bruise appeared on my right bum-cheek. And I decided to visit Mark in prison. The tube would be the quickest and cheapest option. But I couldn't take the tube so I took a cab over to the other side of London. Of course, I couldn't afford it.

Her Majesty's Prison Wormwood Scrubs was a huge, imposing old building where security was high. I was so nervous going through the gates and then the special double-door system, that the guards thought I was carrying contraband and frisked me twice. Me asking them to avoid pressing me near my bruised buttock only made them more suspicious. But eventually I was cleared and allowed through.

I gave my name and Mark's full name and surname to another guard at a desk. He then checked some papers and proceeded to call a number out over a tannoy-system. I was then led through to a large room which looked like a school canteen. Several guards stood around the perimeter with stern looks on their faces. I was led to a table with a number 5 daubed on it, where I sat and waited.

I stayed there looking around at the other prisoners and their visitors. The atmosphere was tense yet in some way, jolly. Then suddenly a side door opened, and Mark was led through to sit opposite me. He looked pensive, sad and pathetic until he spotted me and then his face lit up.

'Alright babe' Mark spoke breathlessly but with a smile on his face. I was relieved as I'd anticipated he might blame me for his incarceration. I thought he might even refuse to talk to me. But he sat at the table opposite me and shuffled his chair forward.

Then we started to discuss the night that had led to him being imprisoned. Of course, my memories were vivid. While his were hazy with only minimal moments of lucidity. He couldn't even remember kicking me or the telly and said he hadn't known why he'd awoken in prison the very next day, until the officers had told him. But he swore on his mother's life that it would never happen again.

CHAPTER 22

Breakup

A few days later Mark came home and a few days after that, 'Jen, I didn't tell ya that Annie visited me in Scrubs - did I?' he said. I was confused, was that a question? If it was, then it was surely rhetorical! I started to hear my own heart beating in both ears and I had a feeling of lack of control over everything. But my first thoughts were, 'How dare she visit him in prison, she had no right!' I said nothing as he continued, 'I didn't tell ya but I'm telling ya now, she ses she's pregnant'

That was too much. This life was too cruel. She was a Hospital Social Worker. A Social Worker did this to me! She would replace my children with hers. I hated her like I'd never hated anyone.

Then history repeated itself and just as my father had left us to live with his pregnant girlfriend - Mark packed a bag and went off to live with his pregnant girlfriend. A few days later he was back again saying he wanted to be with me, not her. But he didn't stay home that evening. He needed a drink he said. After a few drinks he came home and started shouting at me. Then he put his fist through a mirror and as the blood ran from his knuckles he grabbed me by the throat and smeared his blood all over my face. I guess that's what he wanted to see, my face covered in blood. I don't know, I'd lost all sense of reason, all sense of logic.

I broke free from him and ran out of the flat, screaming. I knocked on a random door and pleaded they let me in. I was terrified that Mark was hot on my heels. The neighbour called the police and while Mark was taken to the Police-Station the same policeman met me at the flat. He stayed and talked to me.

'Jennifer, I've been in the force for a while now. I've seen a few things that I didn't want to see. Look what I'm trying to say is, if you don't get away from him, we're gonna have to come out someday soon and scrape you off the walls! I've seen it before and I know where this is going. Listen to me - you have to get away from him, he's bad news. He's gonna kill you!' The policeman's tone was gravely serious.

'Look I've got no one without him' Tears rolls down my face and dripped on the floor. I could feel the policeman's eyes on me. 'He's got another bird pregnant you know'

The policeman shook his head. 'I don't know how many more reasons you need to finish with him. You're just asking for it, staying with him. Haven't you got anyone who can help you, support you through this, keep you company even?' he continued.

There seemed to be a reoccurring pattern in my life. The lack of love that'd led me to this mess was also holding me in it. 'Surly there's someone, anyone?' he went on.

There was a female student who I'd chatted with one time in the Eddie. She was much taller than me with dyed red hair. She'd told me her name was Caz. She was super-clever and a bit of a maths-wiz by all accounts. But she was usually drunk as a skunk. The conversation had taken place on a night when Mark had held me up in the pub and nearly strangled me, while half of the punters had pleaded with him to let me go. Before dropping me, he'd given me a punch on the nose which resulted in a nosebleed, and I'd ended up being counselled by Caz. She'd told me, with no uncertainty, to finish with Mark but she was clever enough to know that I'd need support and didn't have any. So, she'd offered for me to stay with her in her student digs, until I was strong enough to go back to the flat and be alone. I hadn't thought much about the offer at the time as I really didn't know her well. Maybe it was just alcohol talk and maybe in the cold light of day she'd take back her invite. And anyway, I couldn't imagine ever being strong enough to finish with Mark or to live on my own at the flat. But it was my only hope.

'I know, I know, ok, ok I will try, I'll see if I can find this girl, Caz, from the pub,' I said.

'Ok good, we'll put a police injunction on Mark now, that means, he can't come down this street, he's not to speak to you and if he sees you out, he's to cross over the street if he sees you coming towards him, but this will only work if you stick to it too' The policeman looked so serious.

I had a rough idea where Caz lived and thankfully, next day I found her. I felt embarrassed to talk about it all, in the cold light of day. I felt like I was homeless again and in a vulnerable state, where she held all the cards and I held none. She could just say 'no' for whatever reason and I would feel her rejection on top of everything else. But she said yes. She was in total agreement about me staying with her for a few days or as long as it took.

I made arrangements for Mark's things to be taken to his mum's house and I felt terribly guilty and sorry for him. I didn't know what was right or wrong anymore and was still unsure about my actions but I continued. The injunction was instigated and I went to stay with Caz for a few days. We drank tea and I cried and we talked a lot. The panic attacks kept coming and going. If it hadn't of been for her, I never would have completed the breakup.

It took a tremendous amount of willpower.

After the breakup I passed Mark several times whilst out and about. It was always nerve-wracking but he always crossed over and we both avoided eye contact. I guessed we both had had enough and knew it was for the best that it was over. The chance to replace our babies was lost forever and Annie went on to have a healthy son (followed a year or so later by a healthy daughter.)

It was Spring and I was living alone in the full throws of a complete nervous-breakdown but I didn't know what was happening. I thought I was claustrophobic when I felt breathless. I was avoiding all forms of public transport and I'd spent food money on taxis. Then I'd started to have the same feeling of panic whist queuing at the supermarket and now I was even getting it while at home alone. The attacks were happening several times a day. I was in a bad way. I feared everything. If I was out, I'd run home to safety and then I felt scared there too. I constantly thought someone would break in and kill me or the building would collapse and crush me or an aeroplane was about to land on the building. When the panic came my heart beat so fast and I felt so faint that I truly believed I was dying.

I was severely under-weight; I was buying a half bottle of Bacardi most evenings to drink alone. And I was back to smoking a pack of twenty a day. This was a kind of suicide. A long, slow and painful end.

One day I'd been lying down on the living room floor, petrified and unable to move for half an hour. When I managed to sit up I grabbed my door keys and ran to the doctors. The receptionist saw the state I was in and she grabbed a doctor who made arrangements to get me straight into emergency psychiatry.

Now there are good and bad psychiatrists and psychotherapists as I have since discovered - you cannot always be lucky. It's hit and miss. I was at the mercy of the medical profession or more specifically - the psychiatric unit. But I was lucky, as lucky as anyone can possibly be in this dire situation. Within a matter of days, I was passed, as an emergency, to a clinical psychologist called Anne Richardson. I later discovered that she happened to be one of the best in the country at the time.

I had sessions with Anne twice weekly, in which time she managed to build up my trust. She was steadfast, reliable and genuine. I began to believe that she cared about me and because of that I took noticed of what she had to say, like a child listen's to her mother. Over time she explained a lot and made me understand the process of what had happened to me, mentally. I realised that I was depressed and neurotic and that these two ailments often accompany one another. My 'breakdown' was in a way a 'normal' reaction to successive and repeated grief, fear, disaster and worry. Together we drew up a plan which included a combination of talk-therapy and practical steps to conquer the flash-backs and episodes of panic.

After several months of this constant, caring person in my life, I was much calmer. Anne convinced me to quit smoking to give me better overall respiratory health. She said this would help my confidence that I could breathe which might help to prevent panic attacks. She also said to avoid alcohol. And to stay away from Mark. I no longer went to the pub but I had been purchasing Bacardi from the local off-license and drinking at home alone. I wanted to please Anne, like a child might want to please her mother. I gave up the alcohol quite easily. I struggled with quitting smoking and failed several times but in the end I did it.

Then Anne encouraged me to start to look for work.

CHAPTER 23

Employment

I was still young at nearly twenty-three. I wanted a job. A job would solve some of my problems. It would surely help with my chronic loneliness at the very least. I would make friends and maybe meet a decent guy. I hadn't worked for almost three years and felt now, it was time.

I started to regularly visit the nearest job centre. I always located and checked the office jobs section. Then one day I was in luck. British Telecom was having a big recruitment drive. They were looking for several Clerical Officers at their local billing department. Five O'levels including maths and English were required. I decided to apply.

My application didn't look too good as I had a gap in my work history of nearly three years. I mulled over what stories I could tell to fill in the gaps but, in the end, I decided I would tell the truth and quite simply wrote that I had given birth and left the rest of the section blank.

The personnel department must have reached the conclusion that I'd simply taken a career break. To my amazement, I was invited in to interview at headquarters in central London the following week. I had time to consider how I would play the interview.

Still avoiding the tube, I had plenty more time to decide my cause of action on my long bus journey into the centre of London. I decided honesty was the best policy. If the topic of babies or children came up in the conversation then I would quite simply tell the truth and try to keep my answers to a minimum requirement. If I tried to make up some other story, I felt sure I would get all tongue-tied and end up coming across as dishonest.

Soon enough I located the personnel department and after waiting a short while, I was called in to see the interview panel of three. Questions were asked as the panel went through my work history in chronological order. Things were going well. Then the stumbling block as a kind young man asked the dreaded question.

'We notice you've had a career-break over the last two, oh more like three years, I take it that you have a child?' He leaned forward with a kindly smile.

I took a deep breath. 'I had twins'

'Oh lovely!' An older woman interrupted.

'They both died,' I blurted out.

Then there were horrified faces and an awkward silence.

'They were born prematurely and they both died a few weeks later' I continued. I hoped that statement would suffice.

'Oh, oh, that's awful. Ok so I see. So you've obviously taken time off to recover and that all makes perfect sense now. Sorry we had to ask you.' the young man seemed genuinely apologetic for broaching the subject.

After that, the awkward moment passed and the friendly panel wrote a few notes as they swiftly changed the subject onto hobbies. I simply said that my hobbles were 'reading and swimming' to try to include something intellectual and something active. They all gave each other a knowing smile and I wondered how many other interviewees had said 'reading and swimming.' I kicked myself, I really should have thought that one through a little more. But all in all I felt the interview had gone as well as could be expected.

Less than a week had passed when the envelope arrived with a letter offering me a job as Clerical Officer in the Customer Billing department. I was thrilled although understandably apprehensive. It'd been a while since I'd worked and I'd been through a lot.

Another trip into central London was required for some official paperwork and a photo identification card to be produced. I was informed that I was to start my new job at 9am the following Monday at the local office in Forest gate which was thankfully within walking distance of my address.

Come the start day, I was overwhelmed with nerves but also enthusiastic for the first time in a long while. I was determined to show my self-resilience and not to let my history bite my back forever. This was the first day of the start of my life. I would not let my misfortunes dictate my future. I still had some hope. But had I now been programmed with a malfunctioning spirit? If I had, I vowed to fight it.

The office-block had seven huge floors, six of them were whole offices and the top floor housed the canteen. I was needed on the fourth floor. My immediate manager's name was Ian, a middle-aged blond man who seemed nice enough. Every one of the other nine members, of what was to be my team, were really welcoming and friendly. That was a relief.

There was a pretty Asian girl called Meena, who I was to spend the day with. She had the longest, thickest hair I'd ever seen. She was funny and kind yet I detected a sadness behind her big brown eyes. I guessed everyone had their difficulties in this world.

Meena showed me the fire exits and the toilets. I had my own desk already but I pulled my swivel chair up next to her so as to learn what was involved in the day to day running of the billing department. At lunchtime Meena took me to the canteen where the food was reasonably priced and quite delicious. We chatted and got along well. She naturally asked about my previous employment and I kept it simple by telling her I'd worked as an office temp. I simply talked about the finance office job I'd worked at three years earlier as though it'd been more recent. This way none of my new colleagues needed to know anything about my real story and I could start afresh and in peace. It was all going very well and I felt comfortable in my new surroundings.

After lunch-break, Meena and I sat back down at her desk.

'You ok Jenny? Did you have a nice lunch?' The boss, Ian, shouted over to me in front of all the others.

'Yes, thank you' I smiled politely as I replied.

'How are the kids?' He continued.

'What' My heart dropped.

'Your twins? How are they?' He said, his face full of anticipation for my reply.

The whole team were turning their heads in my

directions and my heart just dropped further. I was backed into a corner and had no option but to lie.

'Oh, fine thanks' I was stunned like a rabbit in headlights. I turned on my swivel chair to face the desk so as my back was facing Ian.

'You didn't mention you had twins! How old are they, boys or girls? Meena enquired with an inquisitive yet confused look on her face.

I felt myself sinking down in my chair. I looked at my handbag down on the floor, at my feet. I was shaking. I felt Meena staring at the side of my face.

'You, ok?' she said, her perplexity increasing.

'Yes, I just need to go to the toilet' I announced.

I grabbed my bag and my cardigan and made for the exit. I walked quickly out of the office and straight to the Ladies toilets on the same floor. As quickly as I could, I entered a cubicle and sat down, head in hands.

'Oh no, oh God no, don't cry, don't cry!' I said to myself, I was completely overwhelmed with a multitude of thoughts and emotion including embarrassment. I tried to think of how to handle this immediate crisis. Then the tears started to run down my face. 'I'm leaving, I have to get out'

'Jenny, you ok?' Meena had followed me into the Ladies.

'Yeah, I'm fine,' I did a good job of managing to hide

the feeling in my voice, 'you go back in, I'll be in, in a minute'

'Ok' her voice trailed off as she left the toilets.

'Thank God,' I said to myself, 'I'm leaving here.'

When I was sure no one else was in the Ladies, I came out of the cubicle. Lunch break was over and everyone was back at their desks. I splashed some cold water onto my face as I looked in the mirror. I was pink and blotchy from crying and my black mascara had run over my cheeks. I put my cardigan on and then quickly grabbed my bag and started my way down the internal staircase. There was no way I could risk the elevator in this condition. I was at high risk of panic attack.

I needed to get out of the building as quickly as possible, so as no one would see me in this state. I couldn't work here now. It was such a shame as I'd really enjoyed my first day up until that point. And the wage was reasonable. But what else could I do but leave? I couldn't start off on my first day telling everyone my sad business. I didn't want to be the gossip of the office. But I guess by now, I already was! And I couldn't pretend I had children at home either. The personnel department had obviously told Ian I had kids. Oh I just didn't know what to do. I had to leave.

I walked down a few more steps and then stopped and looked out of the window at all the people down below on the street. From this height they looked like a colony of ants. 'I'll be out there in a minute and I won't have to give this place a second thought' I said to myself. 'But I want to work here!' I was in such a turmoil.

A drop of maturity and defiance entered my bloodstream and suddenly I turned around and ascended the stairs. As I reached the fourth floor I stopped and got my breath back for a moment. I rubbed under my eyes with the hope I'd removed any smudged mascara. Then I entered the office and marched straight up to the boss.

'Ian, can I have a word with you please?' I spoke

'Yes sure, oh, you mean in private?' He replied.

Most of the team were looking over now. Meena knew that something was going on and looked really concerned and confused.

'Yes, please' I said.

We got just outside of the office and next to the landing of the stairs when I started talking.

'Ian, you know you asked me if I had twins, well I did but they died, they were born prematurely - a boy and a girl. The boy died aged five weeks and the girl died aged seven weeks. They never left their incubators. They were born too early, and they struggled to live but couldn't survive.' Ian looked ashen as I continued, 'I told them at the interview, I told them all about it and I told them that they died so I don't really know what's going on' I shook my head and looked down at the plain blue, industrial carpet on the ground.

'Oh my God Jenny, I'm so sorry. Those idiots at personnel! Somebody has made a right balls-up!' Ian had a horrified look on his face as he continued. 'You see what happens is, when we get a new member of staff, personnel send over a brief bit of imfo' just to introduce the new member of staff to me. Obviously the person given the responsibility for sending a little information over about you has not done their job properly. They've obviously skimmed through your application and now look at the mess they've made, I'm so sorry, this has never happened in all my twenty years of working here. They normally double check everything thoroughly but you seemed to have slipped though the net,' Ian's voice was just becoming all mumbled in my head as he started saying something about the 1984 data protection act and confidentiality. I really didn't care, I still wanted to leave.

'I don't think I can stay now Ian, it's just all too embarrassing.' I felt excruciatingly awkward.

'You're not going anywhere.' Ian insisted, 'we need you on this team, you're not going through the interview process just to leave on the first day cause of some bloody idiot in personnel, come on, we can work this out.'

I hesitated for a minute. Walking back into the office was the last thing I wanted to do at this moment. I'd have preferred to have jumped out of the fourth-floor window only the windows didn't have an option to open. But at the same time, I didn't want to walk out on this fresh start in life. So, I nodded and the two of us walked back into the office together. Everyone looked up. That was such an awkward moment.

Ian insisted Meena spend the rest of the day showing me around the building again. She was also instructed to get me a coffee in the canteen. I guess this allowed Ian time to brief the others on the situation by telling them never to mention my twins to me again. I'm sure he also contacted the personnel department and made sure someone got a good telling off.

Meena hadn't heard the warning about not mentioning it all to me as she'd been out of the office, taking care of me, at the time. So naturally, she asked me all about everything as we sat and drank coffee and then it all came out.

I ended up telling Meena my whole life-story about my parents, my sister, the reasons I left Worcester, everything. But when she got to asking 'Are you still with the father of the twins?' I'd talked enough and so, 'No' was my simple reply. I shook my head.

After that day no one mentioned any of it again. Everyone was kind to me and Ian was an especially good boss. I realised that that day may have been a blessing in disguise. Everyone knew my business against my wishes but at least now I didn't have to worry that the story would one day pop up when I least expected it. Perhaps it was better to be out in the open.

One lunchtime, during my first week of my new employment, I popped out to the local high street and as I was waiting to cross the pelican crossing, I noticed Sally, the social worker, was standing next to me. Her smile beamed at me as we greeted one another. It had been almost a year since I'd been taken off of her priority list. Our final meeting had taken place at my flat where I'd told her that Mark had gotten Annie pregnant. I'd been understandably devasted. Both Sally and Annie were hospital social workers, but they were stationed at different east-London hospitals, so they hadn't known eachother, at that time anyway.

We exchanged greetings and then as the traffic stopped, we started to cross the busy road together. Sally seemed animated as she began, 'I met Annie and the baby last week, oh he's such a gorgeous little thing!' I was shocked at her remark. At the other side of the road, all I could think of to say was, 'ok' as I frowned and shuck my head. I was confused as to why Sally, of all people, would hurt me with this line of conversation!

Then we went our separate ways. On my walk back to the office I surmised that Sally had spoken without thinking. As an east London social worker, she certainly would have had her plate full of a variety of dysfunctional and sad cases. She'd always been so nice to me, like my saviour in a way. I'm sure she never meant to hurt me. Her head must have been full of other complicated life-stories.

Sally had been taken by surprise when she'd bumped into me, and her subconscious had connected me to a woman and baby she'd only recently met. I don't know how or why they'd ended up having a liaison. But I imagined Annie taking her new-born in to show him off at work and somehow social workers from nearby hospitals had all been invited to the celebration. I could picture the balloons, the flowers, the excitement. It was a bitter pill to swallow especially as I cared so much about Sally and thought she cared so much about me. I felt a kind of disloyalty there but I really didn't know the reasons or the circumstances.

I bet, seconds after our brief encounter Sally had realised her mistake. But she never had the opportunity to apologise or to explain as I never saw her again. So, I made up her explanation here. I tried to forget about it all as it rattled around in my head, on my way back to the office.

CHAPTER 24

Emptiness

There was a lot to learn in my newfound employ-ment. I enjoyed writing letters and dealing with customers directly, on the telephone. Although I struggled with the maths part of the job and the drawing up of bills. In general, I settled in well on the busy office team. While living alone in a flat, surrounded by thousands of unknown people, was incredibly lonely.

Now that I had the basics covered, that is, I had a job and a permanent address, I considered that I should be enjoying life. But I felt an indescrib-able kind of emptiness. I hated spending week-ends alone. And I couldn't seem to arrange any kind of social life. Going back to the Eddie would risk ongoing contact with Mark, an addiction best avoided. And it wasn't easy for me, as a female, to go into a new pub alone. My colleagues, at work, seemed to all have their own social lives and I couldn't seem to break into them. It wasn't for the want of trying.

I seemed to have two choices. The first choice was to give up on life and be as lonely as hell. But I'm no quitter so I went with, what I thought was my only other choice. Looking for love. As a young, dare I say it, attractive, vulnerable, heart-broken, unprotected female, with her own flat - what could possibly go wrong?

One lunch-time, I popped out of the office and bumped into one of the older guys from the Stratford house. He told me Mark was regularly seen propping up the bar in the Eddie and he'd had a telling conversation with him recently. Mark had been blind-drunk, as usual, and he kept repeating this -'Jenny was the love of my life, she was the love of my life'

At first, I found Mark's drunken revelation to be ridiculous, incredulous, unbelievable, ironic and even bizarre. I was still so distraught and angry with him after the way he'd treated me. I blamed him in so many ways. How could he possibly sit there night after night, repeating that I was the love of his life! It made no sense. And - didn't he have a new misses and baby to be getting on with nowadays? But according to the guy from the Stratford house, they were no longer a couple or never had been a real couple!

So, I started to accept this story as true. I knew

Mark had come from a very violent and difficult background. He'd often told me of how his father had beaten him and his brothers when they were little. There was a story of them being in a lift together, they were going up to their council flat, where they lived at that time, in a high-rise block. Mark was aged around ten and he'd been behaving in a typically irritating way that ten-year-old boys do. His father had lost his temper and smashed Mark's head into the walls of the elevator. He'd also beaten his two younger brothers. Mark had the scars to prove it. I guess that's where his violent tendencies came from although he still loved and respected his father. Mark was prone to hitting out due, to his history, while I was prone to hitting in. I guess that's often a male, female divide.

I learned this about arguments. Arguments rarely have much to do with the actual words being spoken, or shouted. They're partly to do with others things happening in a person's life at the time. But mostly, arguments are about our background history. Our past dictates our interpretation of current words being spoken. Our history triggers a hormonal response and a visceral reaction. The more damaged we are the less we hear the actual words being spoken and the more we run on our feelings. None of us come through to adulthood unscathed. Inevitably, we're all victims of our history and we all go on to become victims of ourselves.

Now Mark had to learn to live with the conse-quences of his behaviour, just as we all do. Moving on, I wasn't excusing him but I did feel sympa-thetic and some compassion towards him. Perhaps this was a kind of madness on my part. I always managed to feel empathy for those who'd wronged me. It was only easy for me to hate Annie because I never really knew her. If I had sat down and had a conversation with her, I bet I would have felt sorry for her too.

I could never decide if that compassion was a blessing or a curse. In the end I guess it's both. But it definitely put me in a dangerous position mov-ing forward. I was too confused, too soft and I needed to toughen up but never did.

I could have easily made my way to the Eddie that weekend. God knows I was lonely as hell and desperate for company and affection. I know Mark would have been initially over the moon at my ar-rival. I could have had a few drinks and a laugh. It would have felt so great to feel so special again. To feel that euphoria.

According to that policeman, getting back with Mark would have been a death-wish or at the least, a continuation of a terrible saga. I did consider getting back with him though. Why? Because I had nothing else. But I knew he'd crossed a line, a line that couldn't be uncrossed. But the line he'd crossed wasn't his neglect of me or the infidelity or the disrespect or the beatings, although any of these options should have been enough individually. The line he'd crossed was getting another girl pregnant. The same point at where my mother had drawn the line several years before. But she'd gone on to die of a broken heart, something I suppose I was scared of too.

Giving up smoking and giving up Mark were two big addictions, two really hard habits to break. To this day I don't know how I managed to detach myself from either of them. Quitting both wasn't a matter of self-respect or self-care, I think I only quit them because the psychologist had told me to. I was in such a terrible state of mind, at the time, that I'd just done as I was told, as the brainwashed do. If she'd have told me to go jump off Tower Bridge, at that time, I think I've had done it. Luckily for me, she'd given good and motherly advice which was exactly what I'd needed. But she wasn't my mother and I couldn't continue having her in my life as if she were.

So, I didn't suddenly become a mature level-headed adult. Oh no, life could never be that simple. My head was a tangled mess of grief and all manner of issues, most of which the psychologist couldn't untangle. I wasn't now on the road of healthy sensible life choices. It would be great to say here that I lived happily ever after. But this ain't no fairy tale.

Instead of making my way to the Eddie, that weekend, I decided to make a trip to Crystal Palace. It'd been a few years since I'd lived there and a lot had happened during that time. It was a beautiful sunny day and there was such a good view from the overground train and the busses. I still avoided the tube, which would have been the fastest route. But I was in no rush.

I was in the front seat of the top-deck of a double-decker bus as it pulled up on Crystal Palace parade. I got off and wandered around. The main high street was pretty much still the same and I rere-minded myself of all the old haunts I used to visit with the art students and with Vicky. Some places had changed and some pubs had changed names. But mostly everything was as it had been. I walked down a steep hill and came to Cintra Park on my right.

It's funny how, when you go back in time, you ex-pect to bump into all the old people you once knew. But of course, they were all gone. I walked down Cintra Park and approached the big old Edward-ian houses on my left. I stopped and looked up at number 11. The front door had changed colour but other than that, it was all exactly the same.

Then I made my way up to the far end of the street and passed the ground floor flat where I'd once lived with Irish Catherine. The place was over-grown and the entrance was still at the back, still hidden from view.

Then I suddenly remembered Sunny!! Surely, he

wouldn't still be working at Crystal Palace train station, would he? I thought this would be unlikely but I had to pass by just in case. I could go that way and take the train to make my way back to east London anyway.

The train station had had a radical facelift. It was unrecognisable. The old Victorian façade now had a modern monstrosity joined onto it. It seemed that was the way to go in now so I tentatively walked through. I was looking for Sunny in this new unknown location.

There was an older black guy standing near the 'exit to trains' sign, wearing the new train-guard uniform. I considered I might be letting my imagination get the better of me as I thought it could be Sunny! But as I approached him, he smiled and I was pretty sure it was him!

'Hello, are you Sunny?' I had to ask as I wasn't one hundred percent sure.

'Ya ma name Sunny, that no me Christian name but me nickname Sunny, ya wan sumfin, ya goin train?

'Do you remember me? It's me, Jenny!

He hesitated for a moment and then he said, 'Nah, me no ting'

'I used to come here every day. A few years ago now. It's me - Jenny.' I waited, with a big smile on my face, for the penny to drop.

'Nah me no see ya before' He was still smiling but was yet to remember. I guess I'd gone from girl to woman during these years while Sunny still looked pretty much the same as always.

'You gave me a box of chocolates on my birthday and we used to chat every morning and sometimes in the afternoon too' I persisted. I was confident this would jog his memory. I mean I'm sure he wouldn't have gone to such lengths with other passengers. Surely, I was a special one. Any second now he'd remember.

'Nice ta meet ya darlin yeah doh worry doh worry' Sunny said, as he turned to great another passenger and deal with their enquiry.

I looked back over my shoulder as I smiled and said goodbye then I made my way down the steps to the awaiting train.

It was so surprising and disappointing that Sunny hadn't remembered me. He'd made such an impression on me and I would never forget him. But he'd forgotten me. I suppose he'd seen thousands of passengers in the interim, since I'd gone from that area. But I was disappointed I'd been completely wiped from his memory. I tried to justify it in my head. Maybe he'd smoked too much weed in the last few years or had some other unexplained memory loss. Or perhaps I'd changed so much physically and mentally, beyond all recognition due to my experiences. Or maybe I was just an unmemorable, a nobody.

On the day when I'd moved out from Crystal Palace, to go to live and work in the public house in Victoria, I'd looked for Sunny as I'd passed though the station. But he was nowhere to be seen. Obviously, it was his day off. So, I never said goodbye and perhaps I'd upset him. Maybe he did recognise me bit insisted he didn't. No, that wouldn't have been his style surely.

As I sat on that same train, going towards London Bridge, I almost wished Sunny had pretended to know me but I guess he was the honest type. I tried to convince myself it didn't matter. He was only a train station employee and I was just one of thousands of passengers passing through life, remembered by some and forgotten by the majority.

The train took me into central London and then I made my way out to the east by bus and then another train to the heart of the jungle - in Forest Gate.

Living alone in the concrete jungle in the middle of east London still left me in a precarious position. But it was a definite improvement on being in and out of homelessness. My council flat came with a secure tenancy which meant at last I had a settled place to live. It may not have been in an area which meant anything much to me. It was nowhere near as nice an area as Crystal Palace and it certainly had none of the meaning to me as my hometown of Worcester or my old street of Hollymount. But it was a permanent roof over my head with electricity, gas and hot running water.

If I closed my eyes, I was young again. I was running, yes running up the Malvern hills with my mum, my dad and my sister Carol. We were laughing and joking as the sun shone down on us. We were up the Worcester Beacon, the highest point of the Malvern hill range. From there we could see all over Worcestershire! And we were the happiest family that ever lived.

After a few months of earning a reasonable wage packet, from my new employment, I went to the shops and treated myself to a pair of fluffy pink slippers. They were like ballet shoes with satin ribbons and the pink fluff covered my little toes like candy floss.

Foot-Note.

Several years after the ending of this second book, I had two children - a son and a daughter. Their security, stability and education would be of paramount importance to me. Although I inevitably made an abundance of mistakes, I dedicated my life to them. As a mother, I did what I could with the few resources I had. In the main, they knew I loved them and would never abandon them, no matter what. They knew they always had a safety net with me to come home to. With that knowledge, they were free to try and fail and try again. They could fly high and experience all the world's glory.

My daughter's level of education far exceeded mine. She succeeded in graduating from University with a Degree in Psychology! While my son graduated from the Royal Ballet school and went on to become a world-famous ballet star and Principal Dancer!

Printed in Great Britain
by Amazon